television. The young Wombles think it's great fun but I prefer a quiet life. *Tsk, tsk.*

I am very happy to give my pawprint to this reprint (Bungo insisted I use that joke) and hope you enjoy our adventures as much as we did.

Now I must go because Orinoco has just found today's edition of *The Times*. Of course, he has gone straight to the kitchen to claim his reward from Madame Cholet. I think I heard him muttering something about daisy and dandelion fizz . . .

Carry on Wombling.

Great Uncle Bulgaria
The Womble Burrow
Wimbledon Common

The Wandering WOMBLES

Also by Elisabeth Beresford

The Wombles
The Invisible Womble
The Wombles at Work
The Wombles to the Rescue
The Wombles Go round the World

The Wandering WOMBLES

Elisabeth Beresford

Illustrated by Nick Price

BLOOMSBURY

LONDON BERLIN NEW YORK SYDNEY

Bloomsbury Publishing, London, Berlin, New York and Sydney

This edition first published by Bloomsbury Publishing Plc in November 2010

Bloomsbury Publishing Plc
36 Soho Square, London, W1D 3QY

First published in Great Britain in 1970 by Ernest Benn Limited

FSC
www.fsc.org
MIX
Paper from
responsible sources
FSC® C018072

Typeset by Dorchester Typesetting Group Ltd
Printed in Great Britain by Clays Ltd, St Ives plc, Bungay, Suffolk

3 5 7 9 10 8 6 4 2

www.bloomsbury.com
www.thewomblesbooks.com

Sir Badger,
with my love

CHAPTER I

The Enormous Lorry

The trouble really started on a fine spring morning when Bungo Womble was just returning from work. He had been hard at it for most of the night tidying up his patch of Wimbledon Common and, as a party of schoolchildren had been having a Nature lesson on that very patch only the day before, there was a great deal *to* tidy up.

'Amazing, astonishing, extra-ORDINARY,' Bungo

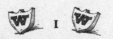

kept muttering to himself as he picked up exercise books and papers, pencils and pens, rubbers and bits of string, gloves and caps, sweet papers and apple cores, orange rind and half-eaten sandwiches. 'Ab-so-lutely EXTRA-ordinary. I don't know how these Human Beings do it, really I don't.'

He often talked to himself while he was out on his own and, although he had been a working Womble for some while, he still hadn't got used to the fact that wherever Human Beings went they always left a trail of bits and pieces behind them. Wombles are the tidiest creatures in the world so, when Bungo saw how beautifully clean this bit of the Common now was, he felt quite proud of himself. He picked up the two very heavy baskets in which he had put all the rubbish and started back across the grass to the front door of the burrow where he lived with his 250 or so relations.

It had been a very wet spring and Bungo's paws left small flat-footed marks,* partly because he was carrying a good deal and partly because he was rather on the stout side. The sun was just starting

* Wombles usually only wear shoes or boots when they know they are meeting Human Beings.

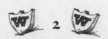

to come out in a pale, half-hearted sort of way and the traffic was already rumbling along the roads which led into London. Even out on the Common Bungo could feel the ground shaking slightly under his paws, and then suddenly the rumbling and the shaking grew worse than ever and Bungo, who was usually quite brave, felt his mouth go dry and his wet fur stick up on end. Even the birds stopped singing and two grey squirrels, who had been shouting rude things at Bungo, shut up and became so still that they looked as if they had been carved out of the trees on which they were poised. It was as though all the creatures on the Common were holding their breath and, of them all, only Bungo had the courage to turn his head to see what was happening.

Travelling quite fast down one of the roads was the most enormous lorry he had ever seen. It was high, it was long and it was wide and it was a silver-grey in colour, and it was making so much noise that it even drowned out the rumble of a jumbo jet thundering across the sky.

'Ho-hum,' whispered Bungo, staring at the thing and shuddering in time to the shivering of the Common. The tree under which he was standing sent down a shower of raindrops which plopped coldly on his fur and suddenly he thought how very nice it would be to be warm and safe and breakfasted down in the burrow. He took to his paws and went running off, panting and snorting until he reached the bushes where the front door was carefully hidden.

'Hallo, hallo, hallo,' said Tomsk, the Nightwatch Womble who was on duty, ticking off the names of returning working Wombles. 'Is it thundering up there?'

'Sort of,' said Bungo, shaking himself violently and then wiping his feet on a mat made of plaited reeds picked from Queen's Mere, a lake on Wimbledon Common.

'What do you mean – sort of?' asked Tomsk, thinking this over. 'It either IS thundering or it isn't. Isn't it?'

But Bungo had already picked up his baskets and gone hurrying off to report to the Workshop where Tobermory was sorting out the things brought in by other working Wombles. Nothing was ever thrown away as useless; even torn paper bags and old bus tickets were put into buckets and soaked with water so that they turned into a really delightful messy kind of stuff. Tobermory always kept one small bucketful for his own use, as mixed with a little cement powder* it was just right for filling in cracks. But most of it went to the Womblegarten where the very small Wombles learnt how to make it into bowls or plates or, more often than not, into rather peculiarly shaped ornaments and toys. It was great fun to do and Miss Adelaide Womble, who ran the Womblegarten, knew that it also taught them how to use their paws neatly.

'My word, you HAVE been busy,' said Tobermory, sticking his pencil behind one ear and putting down his list. 'That's a fine collection of objects, young Bungo. A nice lot of books too, I see. They'll be pleased to get them in the library – always complaining that they're short of books. Off you go to your breakfast then, you've earned it. Nasty thunderstorm that, wasn't it?'

'It wasn't thunder exactly,' said Bungo, putting

* Tobermory had one sack of cement powder left over from the 'Concrete Mixer Expedition', see *The Wombles*.

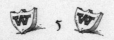

up a paw to hide a yawn.

But Tobermory was sorting through the baskets and putting the things into little heaps while he made a clicking noise with his tongue. So Bungo went off to have a wash and brush-down and then he trotted off to the Common Room where his friend, Orinoco, who was always first in for meals, was keeping a place for him. They stood shuffling and whispering behind their stools until Great Uncle Bulgaria, the oldest and most important Womble of them all, appeared in the doorway and then everybody stood to attention and kept quiet while he made his way slowly to the top table. His fur had turned snow-white with age and he felt the cold a bit these days, so he was wearing his tartan shawl. The moment he sat down, so did everybody else and Great Uncle Bulgaria looked at all their hungry, hopeful faces through his large round spectacles and said, 'Before we start eating there's something I want to ask you.'

Orinoco gave a low moan, for he was aching to begin his breakfast and the smell of fried toad-stools which was wafting through from the

kitchen was making his stomach rumble. Great
Uncle Bulgaria looked at him over the top of his
spectacles and Orinoco tried hard to pretend that
it wasn't him who had made the noise.

'Something I want to ask you,' repeated Great
Uncle Bulgaria. 'Who was it who was making all
that din up and down the passages this morning?'

There was absolute silence while Great Uncle
Bulgaria looked at face after face, his white fur
wrinkled into a frown. Wombles don't tell lies, but
keeping quiet about something is rather different
and everybody soon began to glance at his or her
neighbour, hoping they'd own up quickly so that
breakfast could start.

'Noise? Noise?' said Tobermory, coming into the
Common Room still smoothing down his grey fur
– he was only a few years younger than Great
Uncle Bulgaria and in a few years would be just as
white. 'Noise in the passages? I think it came from
outside. Must have been thunder. Bungo was the
last to report in – he'd know.'

'Please,' said Bungo, 'it wasn't thunder exactly.'

'What do you mean, not exactly?' asked the
oldest Womble.

'Well, it was *like* thunder only it wasn't up in the sky. It was on the new road that leads to Tibbet's Corner.'

Several of the youngest Wombles drew closer together at this frightening idea and Great Uncle Bulgaria's frown deepened.

'Please explain yourself clearly,' he demanded.

'And get on with it, do,' whispered Orinoco out of the corner of his mouth. He would probably faint from starvation in about two minutes, he was sure.

Bungo cleared his throat.

'The noise came from a lorry. A really enormous, ENORMOUS lorry. It was as big as – as big as this room and the kitchen and the Playroom and the Workshop all put together and much higher. It made the Common tremble up and down. It was . . .'

'Enormous,' said Great Uncle Bulgaria. 'Very odd. It even made the burrow shake a bit. Well, I don't suppose it'll happen again. Very well, you may start . . .'

But even as he spoke, the rumbling did start again. It was muffled now by the ground above

8

them, yet it still made the mugs and plates jump on the table and all the knives, forks and spoons jingled. Great Uncle Bulgaria's spectacles jiggled up and down on his nose too and one of the very youngest Wombles giggled nervously.

'Start breakfast,' said Great Uncle Bulgaria very loudly and picked up his knife and fork. The rumbling was drowned out by the noise of stools being scraped nearer the table and an instant hum of conversation, for they all hated having to keep quiet even for a few seconds.

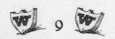

'I don't like it,' said Great Uncle Bulgaria in a low voice to Tobermory. 'There's far too much noise these days out in the world. When I was young you could stand on the Common at dawn and listen to the birds sing. If you try the same thing today, you can't hear a thrush four feet away because of all that dratted traffic.'

'And it'll get worse,' said Tobermory gloomily. 'Hold on a minute, I found a piece in the paper only yesterday.' And he put his paw into the big pocket in the front of his apron and brought out a cutting. 'Yes, here we are. Transport Minister said yesterday in the House of Commons, mumble, mumble, go forward into the future of this new technological age – what a ridiculous word – with better means of, mumble, mumble, ah – containerisation. There!'

'I'm no wiser,' said Great Uncle Bulgaria, mopping up the last of his fried toadstools with a piece of wheatgrass bread.

'I'm not too sure about it myself,' admitted Tobermory, 'but roughly what it boils down to is that goods come to this country in extremely large packing cases, which are then put on these extremely large lorries down at the docks. These lorries are called containers. Because they contain things you see and . . .'

'I'm not a complete fool,' said Great Uncle Bulgaria, feeling rather irritated. 'I get the general idea and what it boils down to, my friend, is that lorries are getting larger and more noisy and now that they've built that new highway, we shall get more than our fair share of them.'

'Can't be helped,' said Tobermory. 'We'll just have to put up with them like the Human Beings do. Perhaps we could wear earmuffs.' And he began to scribble a few pictures of earmuffs on the pad he always kept in his apron pocket.

Great Uncle Bulgaria snorted and went on with his breakfast. He knew that the burrow would stand a great deal of shaking since Tobermory had reinforced it some while ago, but all the same it was not pleasant to look into the future and to realise that from now on they would all have to get used to living with this rumbling roar. So, as soon as breakfast was over, he went back to his own cosy little room and wrapped the shawl more tightly round his shoulders and put his old paws up on a stool and slowly rocked backwards and forwards. He didn't even bother to pick up *The Times* (yesterday's edition), which showed how deeply worried he was.

'Perhaps,' he muttered to himself at last, 'perhaps the Human Beings will have the sense to stop all this container-whatsit nonsense. If it's bad for us it must be a lot worse for them up above ground. They won't be able to hear themselves think – if they ever do think, that is. Yes, they'll put a stop to it.'

He was quite wrong, which was unusual for him, as during the next few days the noise got steadily worse and some of the more nervous young Wombles began having nightmares and losing their fur. Even Orinoco, usually the most placid of creatures, became quite upset when, just as he was about to take a lick of dandelion ice cream in a cornet, one of the lorries thundered past and shook the ice cream clean out of the cornet and down Orinoco's fat stomach.

'This is too much,' he said crossly, trying to bend down far enough to lick up the sticky mess. 'Somebody'll have to *do* something.'

Which was exactly what Great Uncle Bulgaria was saying at the same moment to Tobermory: 'We'll have to take action.'

'What sort of action?' asked Tobermory. 'I could make a barrier, I suppose, and put it up across the road, but that would only stop these container-thingummies for a short time.'

'No, that's no good.'

'Or there are the earmuffs,' suggested Tobermory who was rather taken with this idea.

'No, no, *that's* no good. We shouldn't be able to hear each other talk.'

'What then?'

Great Uncle Bulgaria sat up very straight and looked his old friend steadily in the face.

'We shall have to move,' he said simply.

'Move? Us? But we've lived under Wimbledon Common for hundreds of years. There've been burrows here since any Womble can remember. Move! It's unthinkable.'

'Have you got a better idea?' asked Great Uncle Bulgaria, making a grab for his spectacles as the room shuddered and his spectacles with them.

There was a long pause while Tobermory

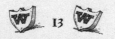

13

scratched his ear with his screwdriver and scowled at the wall. Like his friend, he had spent all his long life in the area of Wimbledon and the thought of leaving it was extremely upsetting.

'No,' he admitted at last, 'I haven't. But I don't like it. I don't like it at all. Besides which, where could we possibly go?'

'Ah-HA,' said Great Uncle Bulgaria, getting stiffly to his feet. 'Exactly, precisely, where? I'm coming to that. Follow me.'

'Where to?' asked Tobermory, who was still dazed by what had been suggested.

'To the library,' replied Great Uncle Bulgaria, who now he had got used to his own astonishing plan was rather starting to enjoy the excitement of it. It made him feel quite middle-aged again. 'Come along, come along. We must start planning the whole operation at once. There's not a moment to lose. We shall take to the open road, old friend, to look for fresh fields and pastures new. In fact, *that* is what I shall call the whole affair, OPERATION WANDERING WOMBLE. OWW for short. From now on you will refer to this business as OWW until I issue an official statement. Well, are you coming or are you going to sit there all day with your mouth open?'

And Great Uncle Bulgaria went hobbling out of the door at a surprising speed for one of his age, leaving Tobermory, his mouth still open, to follow him.

CHAPTER 2

OWW

The library was the only place in the burrow where the youngest Wombles were expected to keep absolutely quiet all the time, which may have been the reason why so few of them used it. It was a smallish room almost entirely lined with shelves and as those shelves were completely filled with books, magazines, comics and news-papers, all of them collected from the Common at

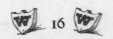

one time or another, it shows just how careless Human Beings are with their belongings.

Great Uncle Bulgaria looked hopefully at the reading desk where the latest edition of *The Times* was always laid out for him if anybody had found one yet, but it was still empty. So he glanced round instead to find out who else was present. There were only two other Wombles in the room, one of whom was Tomsk who was sitting at a desk reading very slowly and carefully and saying the words silently to himself as he went. This was rather surprising as Tomsk was not at all clever and when he wasn't working he spent the rest of his time playing games, at which he was extremely good, but he had never been much of a reader. Great Uncle Bulgaria who, like all the other Wombles, had a great deal of curiosity, shuffled over very quietly to see what the book was. It was called:

Advanced Golf
No. 2
The Putt

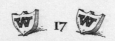

'Ho-hum,' said Great Uncle Bulgaria to himself and beckoned the second Womble who was sitting perched on the top of a flight of steps, busily arranging some of the books which had been brought in only last week. He was rather a small-sized Womble called Wellington and he wore very large, round spectacles. Although like all the others he loved eating, he loved reading even more and sometimes completely forgot to go into meals and had to make do with snacks from the trolley, so he was if not exactly thin, not exactly fat either. As he climbed down the steps and reached the floor Great Uncle Bulgaria poked him in the stomach with his stick and said quietly, 'Not getting enough to eat, young Womble? Can't have that.'

The Womble shuffled his paws and looked down at the ground. He was rather shy and not too sure of himself and he had been such an awful failure when he was first sent out on Common-tidying duty that he was certain that all the others secretly despised him. The trouble was he would suddenly start thinking of something interesting and then completely forget where he was or what he was supposed to be doing, and on his second time out he had wandered away from the patch he had been given and when he didn't return on time, a search party had had to go out looking for him. He had finally been discovered sitting on the very edge of the Common, gazing at the traffic with two empty baskets by his side. The job in the library suited him perfectly as there was hardly anybody to notice if he did go off into a dream and he liked being surrounded by so many books.

'Sorry,' he whispered now.

'So you should be, young Wellington. We Wombles are going to need all our energy and strength in the hard months ahead,' said Great Uncle Bulgaria, who was rapidly becoming more and more like a general at the head of his troops. 'Now then, I'm going to take over this library and turn it into my Operations Room.'

'Has somebody hurt themselves?' asked Wellington in a distressed voice.

'Not *that* sort of operation. Ah-HA, here's Tobermory. Tomsk, out of here.'

Tomsk took not the slightest notice, but went on quietly to himself '. . . down on the ground to

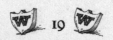

get the lie of the land. This is very im-port-ant as . . .'

'He doesn't hear anything except the dinner bell,' said Wellington. 'He has to think so hard when he reads, you see.'

'Better leave him alone then,' grunted Great Uncle Bulgaria. 'Push those two reading desks together and get me all the maps of the British Isles you can find and lay them out. Tobermory, I want a large board to hang up on the wall.'

'What for?' asked Tobermory grumpily. He felt upset and out of sorts and he hadn't caught any of Great Uncle Bulgaria's enthusiasm yet.

'Daily Orders. Notes. Campaign Dispatches,' said Great Uncle Bulgaria grandly. Tobermory went off muttering and Wellington pushed the desks together and got out the maps while Great Uncle Bulgaria hummed softly to himself and Tomsk slowly turned another page. As soon as all the maps Wellington could find were laid out, Great Uncle Bulgaria began to sort through them while the young Womble watched him anxiously. Of course he hadn't the faintest idea what was going on and it all seemed very odd to him, but he was too shy to ask and he nearly jumped out of his fur when Great Uncle Bulgaria said suddenly, 'Not much green stuff left, is there?'

'Green stuff?' said Wellington timidly.

'Open land, common land. Look at that and that.' Great Uncle Bulgaria waved a paw over the maps of Surrey, Sussex and Kent. 'All being turned into houses and roads and estates and goodness knows what else. In the years to come there won't be any fields left, but I shall be dead and gone by then so it won't worry me.'

'I'm sure you won't,' said Wellington, who like everybody else was sure that Great Uncle Bulgaria would last for ever and Wombles do, in fact, live to a very great age. 'Can I help – or – or,' he swallowed nervously, 'would you rather I went away?'

Great Uncle Bulgaria stopped studying the maps and looked at Wellington over the top of his spectacles. He knew all about Wellington's shyness, which was a most unWomble-like weakness, and he also knew that Wellington probably felt a bit lonely and left out of things generally. So he thought very hard for a moment or two and then said very slowly and solemnly, 'No, I'm going to need you, young Womble, and I am going to trust you with a great secret.'

At these words a shiver went right down Wellington's small back and he felt larger and more important than he had ever done in his short life. He straightened his rather bent shoulders – he'd got those from being hunched over books so much – and stood stiff as one of the library shelves. A faint rumbling noise filled the air and the spectacles of both Wombles slid down their noses.

'That,' said Great Uncle Bulgaria, dramatically pointing at the shivering ceiling with his stick, 'is the enemy. We are peaceful creatures, and we can't go on living with that – that man-made thunder. There is only one thing left for us to do and that is . . .'

'Your board,' said Tobermory, coming in sideways through the door and holding between his paws a large piece of hardboard.

'That is,' went on Great Uncle Bulgaria loudly, 'to find somewhere quieter.'

'*Shh,*' said Tomsk, looking up from his book. He had reached a very long word and was having some difficulty reading it. He recognised Great Uncle Bulgaria and added, 'Oh, sorry. Excuse me, the-or-yit-i-cally. That can't be right.' And he put his paws over his ears and went back to his book.

'He wants us to leave Wimbledon,' said Tobermory, heaving the board against some of the shelves. 'I don't know, it doesn't seem right to me, but then I'm not in charge. I only look after the Workshop. What I think doesn't count.'

'Yes, it does,' contradicted Great Uncle Bulgaria, 'you're my second in command and I shan't be able to manage at all without your help. I depend on you for your support, old friend.'

There was a long pause while Tobermory pretended to be very busy putting up the board. He took his time over it, but Great Uncle Bulgaria watched him patiently and when Wellington opened his mouth to ask a question he was frowned at, so he shut it again. Then, when at last the board was just the way he wanted it to be, Tobermory even more slowly and deliberately took a long slip of paper out of his apron pocket and pinned it up. Written in large letters were the words:

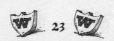

OWW

Daily Orders   Notes   Campaign Dispatches

Great Uncle Bulgaria blew his nose loudly and then put away his handkerchief and said, 'That's all right then. First we have to decide just where we are moving *to*. Wellington, you'd better make notes. We want this whole business carried out in a proper, efficient manner. We're not going to rush into anything.'

Tobermory said something under his breath which Great Uncle Bulgaria was too polite to comment on, but which made Wellington, now fairly trembling with the excitement of being right on the inside of something so important, grin to himself. Their three heads bent together while at the far end of the room Tomsk neatly put away his golf book and then tiptoed out to go and look for his friends Bungo and Orinoco.

'Where've you been?' demanded Bungo. 'We've looked everywhere for you. I wanted to have a game of Hide the Womble and it's no fun with only old Orinoco because he just lies down behind a bush and then goes to sleep.'

'I've been in the library,' said Tomsk, 'reading. A book.'

'Whatever for?'

'I want to improve my golf. Look, this is how you putt.'

And Tomsk, who was the largest Womble in the burrow, got slowly down on the floor and lay on his stomach while Bungo watched him in astonishment.

'I shouldn't go to sleep there if I were you,' said Orinoco, coming round a corner with the crumbs of a cream bun still on his whiskers. Losing his ice cream had upset him so much he had had to go after the tea trolley to get a little something to keep up his strength.

'I'm not sleeping,' replied Tomsk, heaving himself up again. 'I'm studying the lie of the land. It's very important when you putt and . . .'

'Let's go and play now,' said Bungo hastily, for once Tomsk got on to the subject of playing golf he went on and on about it. 'Come on, it's a

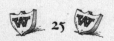

very nice afternoon for us.'

By which he meant that it was cold and damp and grey and there would be very few people on the Common as, not having the Wombles' sensible thick fur coats, Human Beings don't like chilly March evenings. Bungo enjoyed the game very much indeed as he was by far and away the best at it for Tomsk was too large to hide properly except in a very big bush and Orinoco was too lazy to hide carefully. It was also a splendid way to get up a really good appetite for the evening meal and when Bungo had caught Tomsk three times and Orinoco five times and had not been caught at all himself, he decided that it was time to go home.

'I do like Wimbledon Common,' he said as they made for the burrow. 'It's just about the best place in the whole world.'

'It's not bad,' agreed Orinoco, who was walking very fast for him as he was sure he could already smell chocolate and nettle pudding.

'It'll be nasty leaving it,' said Tomsk sadly.

'Why should we leave it?' asked Bungo.

'I don't know,' replied Tomsk. 'But we are. At

least I think we are. Ask Wellington – he knows all about it.'

'Knows about what?' asked Bungo, seizing his friend's arm and shaking him.

'Leaving,' said Tomsk. 'I told you.'

Bungo knew it was no good asking any more questions, because Tomsk had obviously 'got the wrong end of the picnic basket' as the Wombles say, so he sighed heavily and let go and went hurrying after Orinoco who was already burrowing through the bushes to get to their main front door. Bungo had a sort of a feeling that something was wrong somewhere because he'd got that kind of uneasy prickle in his fur, so being a determined creature he decided to get hold of Wellington at the first possible chance. The supper bell had just gone and the moment he was in the Common Room Bungo kept his sharp little eyes on the door. Wellington, he knew, sometimes missed lunch, but no Womble was allowed to go supperless to bed so he was sure to turn up in a minute.

They all stood whispering and shuffling behind their stools waiting for Great Uncle Bulgaria and

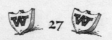

only keeping quiet for a second or two when the burrow shook with the now familiar rumble; and then another odd thing happened for it wasn't Great Uncle Bulgaria who went up to the top table, but Madame Cholet who was the head cook. She had put on her best apron in honour of the occasion and when she took her place there was a great buzz of conversation. It was very rare for Great Uncle Bulgaria to have supper in his own room and Bungo said anxiously to Orinoco, 'You don't suppose he's ill, do you?'

'No. Probably having a special snack of something-or-other,' replied Orinoco rather thickly as his mouth was extremely full.

'And where's Wellington?' went on Bungo. The prickly feeling in his fur was getting worse all the time.

'In the library, I expect,' said Tomsk. 'Tobermory's there too.'

'Something's wrong,' said Bungo. 'I know it is.' And for the first time in the whole of his life he hardly felt like eating although he did just manage to have a second helping of the chocolate pudding as naturally he didn't want to upset Madame Cholet's feelings by refusing it. However, as soon as the meal was over, instead of going to his bed for a sleep before he started clearing-up work at dawn, Bungo insisted on going to the library.

'I don't want to read anything,' protested Orinoco.

'We're not going there to read,' snapped Bungo, pushing his fat friend ahead of him with one paw and dragging Tomsk behind him with the other.

'They won't let you talk in there, you know,' said Orinoco over his shoulder. 'Don't push so hard – I'll fall over.'

'You'd only bounce if you did,' replied Bungo. 'Here we are. Now I shall find out just what is going on.'

And then he and Orinoco and Tomsk all stopped quite still, for pinned across the door was a large notice which said:

OWW OPERATIONS ROOM
No admittance except on official duty
Signed: Officer in Chief
BULGARIA COBURG WOMBLE

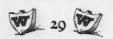

'Well,' said Bungo.

'What does it mean?' asked Orinoco.

'Told you!' said Tomsk. 'But you wouldn't believe me. You never do,' and he sighed. 'What shall we do now, Bungo?'

CHAPTER 3

Fresh Fields and Pastures New

It was three dreadful days before Bungo's now consuming curiosity was to be satisfied. He didn't believe, as Tomsk had come to do, that a splendid new game was being invented, perhaps something like Wombles and Ladders only even more exciting. Or, as Orinoco now thought, that larger kitchen, larder and pantry quarters were being planned.

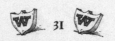

'It's not something nice. I know it isn't,' said Bungo. 'I can feel it inside me.'

'All I ever feel inside me is empty,' said Orinoco and then added thoughtfully, 'and sometimes full, of course.'

'Well, Great Uncle Bulgaria seems quite happy,' said Tomsk in his slow way, 'happier than he was two weeks ago. So it can't be something nasty.'

It was quite true for Great Uncle Bulgaria was very busy these days, either talking to Tobermory in a low voice, or vanishing into the library with a pile of papers under his arm and on his evening stroll into the outside world he had taken to wearing a sort of cap with red material sewn round it on a band. And, Bungo had noticed, every time the burrow rumbled and shook, Great Uncle Bulgaria, instead of muttering and frowning to himself, only waved his stick at the ceilings and smiled in a most mysterious manner. Tobermory, too, had changed for he had actually handed over his precious Workshop to another Womble and was only on duty there for a few hours during the afternoon, and even then his mind appeared to be on different things and he would vanish into his own small storeroom at the back and there would be odd bangings and whirring sounds.

Bungo, who absolutely hated being left out of things, decided to track down Wellington and somehow get the whole truth out of him. He managed to catch him by lying in wait round the corner from the library, or Operations Room as it was now called, and springing out just as Wellington gave a knock on the door. It wasn't an ordinary knock either. It was two quick taps, then a pause and then two more taps. He had just done the fourth one when Bungo caught him.

'*Whoops* – look out,' said Wellington, making a grab for the papers which he was carrying and had nearly dropped. 'Do be careful, Bungo!'

Bungo blinked for usually Wellington treated him with great respect and didn't speak to him sharply like this. But then even Wellington had changed these days and was going round with an important air and his shoulders set back.

'Sorry,' said Bungo. 'I say, look here, Wellington, old friend, can I have a word with you?'

Wellington glanced at the enormous wristwatch he now wore and shook his head.

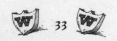

33

'Sorry,' he said in his turn, 'but I'm on duty at 22.00 hours. Musn't be late, you know, or I shall find myself on standing orders.'

'Standing WHAT?' said Bungo, staring.

This strange new language made him feel more out of things than ever.

'Orders,' said Wellington. 'The Officer Commanding is very particular.'

'Oh See?' said Bungo faintly.

The door was opened a crack and Tobermory's face, or at least part of it, appeared.

'Password?' he said in a low voice.

'Pastures New,' Wellington whispered back.

'Come in, friend,' said Tobermory and the door was opened a further few inches and Wellington, being fairly slim, was able to slip through and Bungo found the door not only shut in his face, but also locked.

'Who was that?' asked Great Uncle Bulgaria, looking round from the map he was studying.

'Bungo Womble,' said Wellington, drawing his heels smartly together.

'Ho-hum, Bungo. It *would* be,' said Great Uncle Bulgaria. 'All right, Wellington, give me those

reports. Bungo, eh? Ho-hum.'

If Bungo had been allowed into the Operations Room he would have been even more astonished than he was at this moment. Maps and charts now hung from all the shelves and the board was covered in neatly written papers. At one end of the room there was a large map which Wellington had drawn very carefully. It showed the whole of the British Isles and several bits of it had been coloured green and had the letters FF or PN*

* Fresh Fields and Pastures New.

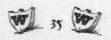

written on them in red. At the bottom of the board were four very large pins, the heads of which were also bright red as they had had pieces of red felt stuck to them. As Great Uncle Bulgaria was also wearing his cap with the red band, the effect overall was extremely colourful.

'Ah-HEM,' said Great Uncle Bulgaria, clearing his throat and rapping on one of the desks with his stick. 'Attention please. I have now reached a decision. We shall strike north and east. Here and here!'

He whacked the big map with his stick and Tobermory said anxiously, 'I say, look out, it's only pinned, you know.'

'North and east,' repeated Great Uncle Bulgaria, ignoring this remark but tapping the map more lightly. 'This means that we shall need two scouting parties.'

'Two?' said Wellington, looking up from his notes. He was trying to learn speed writing, but although he was clever enough he had very little spare time these days and as Great Uncle Bulgaria would talk faster and faster, Wellington often got left behind.

'Two,' repeated the old Womble. 'One pair of scouts will go off – er – scouting, so to speak, to look for a suitable Womble home, while the other pair will stay here as reserves in case there is an emergency.'

'What sort of emergency?' Tobermory asked.

'How should I know until it happens?' snapped Great Uncle Bulgaria. 'You can't say next week there will be an emergency on Tuesday morning at half past ten. An emergency is something unexpected like an earthquake or the roof falling in.'

Tobermory put back his grey head and looked searchingly at the ceiling. He was very proud of this burrow for it was under his direction that it had been almost entirely rebuilt and every nail and every piece of plaster meant a great deal to him.

'It won't,' he said, 'it can't.'

Wellington's pencil went scribble, scribble, scribble over the page of his notebook for he had been told to write down everything that was said at these secret meetings. He didn't know quite why, but Great Uncle Bulgaria had said solemnly that it was important to do so, and that was that.

Flip, the page went over and Wellington licked the end of his pencil which was getting very blunt and waited for what was to come next.

'Now we come to the business of choosing the first scouting party,' Great Uncle Bulgaria went on. 'I've given this a great deal of thought and I suggest Bungo and Orinoco.'

'Bungo, yes, perhaps,' said Tobermory nodding, 'but – Orinoco?'

'Yes. It's high time that he started pulling his weight – and he's got plenty of that all right.' There was a snuffling sound which meant Great Uncle Bulgaria was enjoying a small joke and Wellington wrote in brackets: *(laugh, laugh, laugh)*. 'And that he began to think of more important matters than what's for supper. That year we went to Battersea Park for our Midsummer party and I made him my Private Office Womble, he did the job quite well. Besides he and Bungo are good friends and they will balance one another. Bungo still rushes into things with both paws and Orinoco, who is more cautious, will hold him back. They have both been out into the world before, at least as far as Piccadilly Circus, so they know something about the great outside. Well?'

Tobermory was silent for a long time while he absent-mindedly measured the distance from the floor to the ceiling just to make quite sure that nothing *had* moved. Wellington was glad of the break and rubbed his paws together as he was getting writer's cramp. He couldn't help feeling a little sadly how grand and glorious it would be to be chosen as a scout and to have a lot of adventures. But you were either the sort of Womble who was picked for that kind of job or you weren't. And Wombles who couldn't even clean up a small piece of Common without getting lost obviously couldn't ever be made into scouts.

'Yes, very well,' said Tobermory suddenly. 'Bungo and Orinoco it is. But they'll have to go into training. That's odd.'

'Training, yes, I was coming to that. You will be in charge of that, Tobermory. You got Orinoco's weight down before when you made him that special bicycle. Now you must get it down again. What's odd?'

'The ceiling is an inch and a half lower than it used to be. I'll have to work out some exercises and things for them to do, early morning runs and so on. Orinoco won't like it, you know, he won't like it at all,' and Tobermory's rather serious face broke into a smile at the idea of tubby Orinoco running.

'He'll *have* to like it,' replied Great Uncle Bulgaria. 'I shall see them both at 09.00 hours tomorrow. The meeting's now closed.'

He took off his cap and Wellington put away the notebook in a box with a lock and key and OWW TOP SECRET painted on the lid. Then he went to look at the map to try and work out which north and east Bungo would be going to, but there was a great deal of both so he gave it up as a bad job and turned off the light and followed the other two out of the room just as Tobermory was saying, 'By the way, who will make up the second pair?'

'Ho-hum,' replied Great Uncle Bulgaria, putting one white paw to the side of his nose, 'that, for the moment, is Top Top Secret, old friend,' and he winked mysteriously before going on his way to his own room for a final nightcap of hot blackberry juice.

So it was that the following morning a very

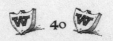

surprised Bungo and Orinoco were informed that as soon as they had finished breakfast they were to report to the Operations Room.

'Now what have we done?' said Bungo anxiously, remembering how he had just happened to have propped up three of the legs of Tomsk's bed and how very funny Tomsk had happened to look as he bounced off it on to the floor.

'I haven't done anything,' said Orinoco virtuously. 'I just hope whatever-it-is doesn't take long as I do want a nice forty winks.'

They smoothed down their fur, cleared their throats and knocked on the door which was opened by Wellington.

'Password . . .' he began.

'Pastures New,' replied Bungo promptly. He had an excellent memory when he cared to use it.

'I was just going to tell you,' said Wellington, 'password for even dates is Fresh Fields. Go on, say it.'

'But you've said it,' objected Orinoco.

'Yes, but I'm inside and you're outside.'

'Fresh Fields then,' said Bungo.

'Advance friends and be recognised,' said

Wellington, opening the door further.

'You must want new specs if you can't see us from there,' said Orinoco. 'It's us, you know. Orinoco and Bungo,' and he waved a paw in greeting. Wellington gave up the unequal struggle to try and explain and stepped back smartly and clicked his heels together.

'Number One Scouting Party reporting, sir,' he said and shut the door and locked it again. Bungo and Orinoco looked about them at the maps and the noticeboard and then at Great Uncle Bulgaria who had changed his tartan shawl for a jacket with brass buttons and red tabs on the collar. He was also wearing his new cap and his two pairs of spectacles and he was writing busily at a desk with Tobermory standing behind him. He didn't seem to notice that Orinoco and Bungo had arrived, so they shuffled their paws and nudged each other in the ribs and opened their eyes very wide to show each other how very strange all this was.

'Quiet. Stand to attention,' barked Great Uncle Bulgaria without looking up and the two young Wombles jumped violently and did as they were told. They were practically bursting with curiosity, but they didn't dare to open their mouths. Great Uncle Bulgaria handed the paper to Tobermory and then sat back and gazed at them for some seconds. Then he leant forward and said, 'I have something extremely serious and important to tell you both. You may stand at ease with your paws apart. Nothing I say must go further than this room. Is that understood?'

Bungo and Orinoco nodded violently. Their fur was now standing up on end and their eyes were as round as buttons. There was a distant rumbling sound and both pairs of Great Uncle Bulgaria's spectacles slid down his nose.

'Now then . . .' he said.

It was over half an hour before Bungo and Orinoco fully grasped exactly what was going to happen to the Wombles and the part that they were going to play in OWW. Bungo felt excited and rather nervous and Orinoco was torn between feeling very important and frankly terrified. Wellington was two pages behind in his notes and his spectacles had misted over and Tobermory was starting to wonder all over again if the whole plan could ever work.

'You will be taken off Common-tidying,' said Great Uncle Bulgaria, 'and I shall announce that like Tobermory, Wellington and myself you have been posted to Special Duties. Or SD as we shall now call them. From this moment you will be OWW, SD 4 and 5. You will start your training at 14.00 hours. Tobermory will be your instructor. Any questions?'

Bungo, who was hastily working out what time 14.00 hours was on his paws, shook his head, but Orinoco, who didn't at all care for the word 'training', timidly asked what it meant.

'It means getting you fit, my lad,' said Tobermory who had found a book called:

Keep Fit for Beginners

He had sat up reading it for two nights running and had thoroughly enjoyed picturing Orinoco doing some of the exercises. He had tried a couple of them himself and his back paws still ached a little.

'Ooo-er,' said Orinoco, who didn't like the glint in Tobermory's eye. For two buns Orinoco would

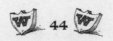

there and then have asked to be excused from the whole business, but somehow with Great Uncle Bulgaria watching him over his spectacles and Wellington writing down everything that was said, he didn't quite like to. There was a bit of a silence and then Great Uncle Bulgaria nodded and said, 'Right. Remember, not a word to anyone. Straight off to bed, the pair of you. Dismiss.'

For once in his life Bungo did exactly as he was told, but Orinoco, who in spite of an excellent breakfast had a strange sinking feeling in his stomach, lingered further and further behind until he caught sight of the mid-morning trolley. He had two buns, one cake and six biscuits and then went slowly to his bed, still munching.

Being a brave explorer was one thing. Keeping fit quite another.

'Oh dear, oh dear, oh dear,' murmured Orinoco to himself and settled down for forty winks with the crumbs still trembling on his whiskers.

CHAPTER 4

The Great Adventure

It was even worse than Orinoco had imagined it would be. Tobermory was one of those Wombles who once he got his paws into a thing just would not give up. If Great Uncle Bulgaria wanted Bungo and Orinoco to be fit, then fit they would be! He started them off with an hour's practice at Wombles and Ladders, a game which Orinoco had never enjoyed very much as, if when the music

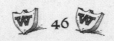

stopped, and you were halfway along the climbing frame, you could, it was true, have five seconds' break. But if you were at the top of a ladder, you had to slide all the way down and start climbing again. And Orinoco always *was* at the top of a ladder, or so it seemed to him. This was followed by what Tobermory called 'simple exercises' like touching the paws without bending the legs. Orinoco just managed to reach as far as his knees. Then there was ten minutes' glorious rest while he lay flat on his back and panted and then, worst of all, there were 'runs'.

'One-two, one-two,' ordered Tobermory, riding along beside them on Orinoco's old bicycle. 'Keep those knees up. One-two, one-two.'

Even Bungo had to admit that by the end of four days of this he was exhausted. Orinoco was too tired to do anything but crawl into his bed and lie there. The trouble was that these days he was hungrier than he had ever been, but Tobermory had put him on a diet and his stomach now rumbled almost as loudly as the giant lorries.

'I don't want to be an SD,' he wailed to Bungo.

'Then go and tell Great Uncle Bulgaria.'

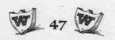

'You know I can't. He'd look at me over his spectacles. Oh dear, oh dear.'

One of the most difficult parts of the whole business was keeping quiet about it, for the Wombles have more than their fair share of curiosity and Bungo and Orinoco were asked at least a dozen times a day what they were up to. Bungo simply ached to tell the others about his important new job, but he didn't dare to as Great Uncle Bulgaria had made them sign a paper entitled:

WOMBLES' OFFICIAL SECRETS ACT

And after they had done it he had told them in a very serious voice that if they told anyone else in the burrow anything at all, they would be in Real Trouble. As this could only mean not being allowed to talk to anyone, which is the worst punishment there is, even poor Bungo had to keep his mouth shut and just look important. Orinoco was too tired to talk anyway.

'Hard luck,' said Tomsk sympathetically. 'I suppose you've both done something wrong and all this exercising is a sort of punishment. Don't worry, old chap,' and he raised a large paw, 'I won't ask what it is you've done. I'd just like to say how sorry I am.'

A kindly, well-meant remark which made Bungo nearly explode with fury. Tomsk patted him on the shoulder and went on in his slow way, 'Although I wish I knew what it was, because I'm fond of exercise myself and I should like it as a punishment. Would you care for a round of golf this afternoon?'

'Can't. Got swimming instruction,' said Bungo shortly and ran off. He had quite got into the habit of running everywhere these days, with his elbows well tucked into his sides and his chin up.

'One-two, one-two,' chanted Tobermory, who was waiting beside Queen's Mere with another useful little book he had got out of the library. Unfortunately some of the middle pages were missing so that it went straight from simple life-saving to advanced diving, but then, as Tobermory so rightly said, Wombles can't be choosers.

'I want you to do two lengths of the Mere,' he ordered. 'Breaststroke now, Orinoco, not Womble-paddle.'

'I can swim already,' grumbled Orinoco, ruffling up his fur for it was raining steadily.

'In you go,' replied Tobermory, taking no notice, and he gave them both a push into the cold, muddy water, startling the ducks who went quacking off towards the banks. 'You never know when a little swimming practice might come in very useful.'

Which as it later turned out was absolutely true, but for the moment Bungo and Orinoco were far too busy keeping the water out of their ears, noses and eyes to think about anything else. Up and down the Mere they went, their small round bodies making funny little humps in the muddy water. They really did swim rather well and Tobermory felt quite proud of them when they at last clambered up on to the footpath and shook themselves vigorously.

'Not bad,' he said. 'Back to the burrow for motor-scooter drill, one-two, one-two . . .'

Just when Bungo reached the point where he felt he would go off, *bang*, if he didn't tell somebody what this was all about, he got his reward. Great Uncle Bulgaria called a meeting of everybody in the Common Room that evening, and even the smallest Wombles came to it with Miss Adelaide keeping a firm but kindly eye on them. They sat on the floor in the front row, pushing and chattering and looking round at all the older Wombles behind them.

'Shh, that's enough, up you get,' ordered Miss Adelaide as Great Uncle Bulgaria, wearing his new uniform, came into the room with Tobermory behind him and with a rather weary-looking Wellington bringing up the rear. Tobermory pinned up the big map and Great Uncle Bulgaria tapped it with his stick.

'Fellow Wombles,' he said, 'I have some important news to tell you. We are very much afraid that a large part of this burrow may have to be closed down. This is because bits of it have begun to sink owing to the enormous amount of heavy traffic which is now passing along the main road. You may have noticed yourself that doors have been sticking and that the floors sometimes shake and tremble.'

A kind of shiver and a long drawn-out sigh of horror passed through the assembled Wombles.

'It's nothing to worry about too much,' said Great Uncle Bulgaria hastily as a very small Womble opened its mouth and began to howl. He glanced at Miss Adelaide who picked it up and rocked it backwards and forwards in her lap until it stopped howling and began to sniff instead.

'Nothing to worry about,' he repeated. 'We shall just have to find somewhere else to set up our home. Fortunately we have in our family two brave, determined and tough young Wombles who are going to search out this home for us. I refer to Bungo and Orinoco who tomorrow are setting out on a scouting party. I've called you all here tonight so that you can wish them good luck.'

And Great Uncle Bulgaria waved his paw to where Bungo and Orinoco were standing looking astonishingly modest for them.

There was a moment's surprised silence and then everybody began cheering and Tomsk started singing:

'For they are jolly good Wombles,
For they are jolly good Wombles,
For they are jolly good Woooooombles and so say all of us . . .'

All the others joined in and there was a great deal of backslapping and paw-shaking and also a great many suggestions as to where new burrows might be found or built. Once they got over the shock almost every Womble began to think it might be rather fun to go and live somewhere else, but some of the older members shook their heads and said that they didn't fancy leaving Wimbledon Common at all. Miss Adelaide and Tobermory had a nice long talk about this, swapping stories about how very much better things had been when they were young and the Common had been as quiet as the country and the only drawback had been the enormous number of rabbits and squirrels.

'And horses,' added Miss Adelaide, taking a very clean handkerchief out of the pocket of her starched apron and wiping the nose of a young Womble who was sniffing with the excitement of it all.

'And horses,' agreed Tobermory. 'I never cared for horses. Too excitable. Handsome, I grant you, if you like a skinny kind of animal, but no brains to speak of. I remember once when

I first started work in ... let me see, was it nineteen hundred and three or four ... ?'

And Tobermory was off again while Miss Adelaide nodded and said 'quite so', and 'yes indeed', and 'how very true, dear me'. And although she listened with the greatest politeness, she also somehow managed to keep a sharp eye on the youngest Wombles, and when she noticed that some of them were starting to get far too excited she glanced at her watch, which she kept pinned to her apron, and clapped her paws and said, 'Time for bed. Line up, please.'

'I don't want to leave Wimbledon much either,' said Tomsk, who had been thinking deeply. 'I like it here because there's the Golf Course and swimming in the summer, and skiing and skating and tobogganing in the winter.'

'You're young, you'll soon get used to somewhere new,' said Tobermory shortly. 'Give me a paw to get this place straight again, young Womble.'

Even as he spoke a very faint idea came into his mind, but he decided to keep it to himself for the time being and to do a little bit of quiet planning of his own.

It was quite one thing to feel like brave heroes with everybody wishing you luck and telling you how splendid you were in the evening, and quite another to face up to what lay ahead in the cold light of early dawn. Bungo and Orinoco didn't feel in the least brave or adventurous as they ate their special breakfast, and it was only instinct which made Orinoco put aside a little something in case his appetite should return later in the day. Then off they went to the storeroom where some clothes had been laid out for them, as it was felt that, though Human Beings rarely seem to notice anything unusual, they might just notice a couple of Wombles in some circumstances. So Bungo and Orinoco pulled on their workman's overalls and rubber boots and gloves — there was always a tremendous selection of gloves from which to choose – and last of all they put on crash helmets and goggles. Then Orinoco caught sight of Bungo and Bungo glanced at Orinoco and they both began to laugh.

'You look awful,' wheezed Orinoco.

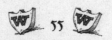

'You look horrible,' gasped Bungo.

'You look fine,' said Tobermory. 'Still a little on the stout side perhaps, but not bad. You'd better have a scarf each too. Red for you, Bungo. Orinoco, you can have the blue one. Now pull yourselves together for goodness' sake.'

Great Uncle Bulgaria looked just a little startled when he first saw them, but Wellington, in spite of being so tired that he could hardly keep his eyes open, had to put both paws over his mouth to stop himself from giggling.

'Ho-hum,' said Great Uncle Bulgaria, 'so the great day has dawned at last.'

'Nearly dawned,' said Tobermory, looking at his watch.

'Here are your orders,' said Great Uncle Bulgaria, handing over an envelope. 'There are two maps, pencils and a notebook, a tape measure, some helpful booklets and a description of the sort of place you are to look for as, don't forget, we need to settle somewhere where we can be of use. We are *working* creatures. Tobermory and I have worked out the route you are to take and some likely places. In this wallet there is some money which you will need for this and that. Try not to spend too much of it on food.' He looked hard at Orinoco as he spoke, but Orinoco's face was so covered up by the goggles and the scarf it was difficult to see what he was thinking.

'And in the notebook,' said Tobermory, who felt he'd been left out of things for quite long enough, 'is the telephone number of a call box near this Common. You will please ring me there at six thirty tomorrow evening to report any news. Also . . .'

'Also,' said Great Uncle Bulgaria loudly, 'there are a pair of remarkably fine binoculars and an old-fashioned camera. It has four shots left on the reel and we have been lucky enough to find an unused film of the right size. It is rather old, but I dare say that won't matter too much. Don't go taking silly pictures of each other. Use the camera to photograph any likely Womble country. I think that's all, so it only remains for me . . .'

'Food,' said Tobermory, producing a very nice little picnic box from his apron pocket. Even through the goggles Orinoco's eyes brightened.

'Only remains for me to say, the very best of luck

and we shall all be thinking of you,' said Great
Uncle Bulgaria very loudly indeed. He held out his
paw and Bungo and Orinoco shook it, feeling
rather shy.

'Yes, rather,' said Wellington, looking up from
his notes and sighing deeply. Although he wasn't
brave or adventurous, it would be wonderful to be
able to stop writing and to go off into the great
world outside, with everybody saying how marvellous you were.

'Come along,' said Tobermory, 'you've got to get
away before the rush hour starts.'

They followed him through the burrow and out
to one of the back entrances where, leaning
against the wall, was the small motor scooter
which Tobermory had been so busy making in his
own little workshop. Bungo had learnt to ride it
quite well, but Orinoco still got fussed over his
paw signals, so Bungo was to be the driver for most
of the way.

'We still don't know where we're going,' said
Bungo, shivering a little in the chill grey air as
Tobermory unbolted the door.

'Sealed orders,' said Tobermory. 'You're to wait

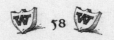

till you get to the other side of the Common before opening them. It's a security precaution. Good luck, young Wombles. Remember your manners, keep your eyes open and use your brains.'

He patted them both on the shoulder, blew his nose and helped them on to the scooter. It seemed to make a great deal of noise and none of them heard the sound of scurrying footsteps until a breathless voice said, 'Hi, I say, hold on.'

And there was Wellington with his spectacles all misted over and with something clutched in one paw.

'It's for you both,' he said, handing over a large object. 'I thought you might find it useful.'

'Oh, you shouldn't,' said Bungo.

'It's jolly kind,' said Orinoco, looking over his friend's shoulder and bumping up and down slightly in time with the thudding of the motor scooter's small engine.

It was Wellington's wristwatch.

'Go on,' he said. 'I'd like you to have it. It loses about five minutes a day and you won't forget to wind it, will you? I must . . .'

And with those words he faded back into the

burrow while the sound of the motor scooter grew fainter and fainter until it merged into the rumble of the early morning traffic at Tibbet's Corner.

'That was a nice thing to do,' said Tobermory, looking out across the Common where his sharp old eyes could just make out the portly forms of returning working Wombles who had been on night duty picking up rubbish.

'Um,' said Wellington and sighed yet again. 'I wish that . . .' and stopped. Tobermory closed the door and bolted it and looked at Wellington's tired, rather sad face and then took out his screwdriver and adjusted one of the bolts which was a bit stiff.

'Well, you know what they say,' said Tobermory, frowning at his handiwork. '*If wishes were horses Wombles would ride*, although I doubt it very much myself as Wombles and horses don't mix. Still there's no *harm* in wishing. How do you get on with Tomsk?'

'Very well,' replied Wellington, rather surprised at this unexpected question. 'I can do things he can't and he can do things I can't.'

'Exactly,' said Tobermory even more strangely still. 'Well, come along, come along. I've got

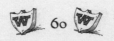

another busy day ahead of me and we haven't had breakfast yet.'

They made their way down the passage, both busy with their own thoughts until Tobermory said abruptly, 'I just hope they'll be all right. I don't know . . .'

And at about the same moment Bungo and Orinoco were spreading out their secret orders, screwing up their eyes to read them in the thin early light. Bungo shook out the map and traced the red line which had been drawn on it.

'Gosh,' he said faintly.

'Oh my,' agreed Orinoco, swallowing.

They stared at each other and then without another word they folded the papers and the map away, and Bungo buttoned them into his overall pockets and started up the engine again. Orinoco clambered on to his pillion seat and grasped his friend firmly round the middle. For a fleeting second he glanced at the nice familiar Common and wondered if either of them would ever see it again. There was a nasty uncomfortable lump in his throat and he was quite sure that he would have done keep-fit exercises for a whole year if only he could be back in the warm, cosy burrow with all his other friends.

'Here we go,' muttered Bungo, and after looking very carefully left and right he drove the scooter neatly into the main road; and within half a minute he and Orinoco had vanished into the early morning mist.

The great adventure or OWW had begun.

CHAPTER 5

Captured

If you are not used to driving it can be a very tiring business and, although both Bungo and Orinoco had been made to practise and practise by Tobermory, it was one thing to go jogging round the Common with only an occasional car, bicycle or horse to watch out for, and quite another to be caught up in main road traffic. At first it wasn't too bad as there was not a great deal of it about, but

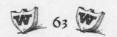

what there was seemed to be mostly enormous and when the scooter became sandwiched between a lorry and a bus at the traffic lights, it was just like being at the bottom of a deep valley. Orinoco's teeth fairly chattered with fright, but Bungo was made of sterner stuff and he stared straight ahead.

Wellington, who had done a great deal of home-work on their behalf, had worked out the simplest route for them to get out of London, but unfortu-nately two difficulties kept holding them up. The first was that Orinoco hadn't yet learnt to read road signs and directions quickly.

'Hold it, slow a bit, I can't quite see – oh yes, that must be the right-hand turn we need. No, it isn't, it's the one after. Oh I say, Bungo,' hitting his friend on the shoulder, 'Bungo, old chap, it was the first right-hand turn, sorry.'

Which meant a great deal of stopping and turning round had to be done. And the second difficulty was that Bungo had pulled his goggles down too far, so that they kept misting over, which meant that he had to stop to polish them.

'We must have gone hundreds of miles,' said

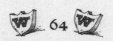

Orinoco when at last they managed to leave London behind and had stopped for a further cleaning of the goggles.

'Thirty,' said Bungo briefly. He was tired already and his shoulder was quite sore from the buffeting it had received. Suddenly, as he sat on the grassy bank, he felt a very lost and frightened young Womble. He was further from the burrow than he had ever been in his life before, and what had started as a great adventure – with himself as the hero – was now a most difficult and lonely task and, he thought miserably, he was going to fail. He just knew he was.

What wouldn't he give at this very moment to hear Tobermory's gruff voice telling him what a silly young Womble he was. Or even to have Great Uncle Bulgaria staring at him through two pairs of spectacles.

Bungo sniffed violently and felt for his handkerchief and at the same moment Orinoco hit him gently, luckily on the unsore shoulder, and said, 'A little bit of something to keep us going, that's what we want!' And he began to undo the packed meal.

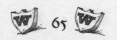

'I don't feel like eating,' said Bungo thickly.

'Don't feel like . . .' Orinoco stared at him in amazement. 'You're travel-sick, that's what it is. All that bumping up and down has upset your stomach. Well, it hasn't upset mine, I can tell you. Mmm, delicious, dandelion rolls and banana mash and chocolate spread and nettle relish and black-berry jam and here – I say, there's no need to snatch, you know.'

'I'll just try a little,' mumbled Bungo, whose mouth was already full.

There was a long period of silence while both of them munched contentedly and, surprisingly enough, by the end of the meal, apart from feeling nicely full, Bungo had also quite recovered his spirits.

'Nothing like a little snack to put you right,' said Orinoco, giving his stomach a satisfied rub. 'Now what we should really do is have forty winks and . . .'

'No,' said Bungo, once again becoming the fearless leader of the expedition, 'we haven't got time. Don't forget we're supposed to be in Scotland by tomorrow night. You can drive for a bit and I'll direct you.'

The next part of the journey was not nearly so wearing as driving through London had been and, although Orinoco didn't drive as fast as Bungo, he had less traffic to deal with and a far less difficult route to follow, so that by the time the evening shadows were drawing across the sky they were north of York and very pleased with themselves.

'It doesn't look like Abroad at all, does it?' said Orinoco wonderingly as they turned off the main road and stopped so that Bungo could get out the map and find a snug resting place for the night.

'It isn't Abroad,' said Bungo. 'You have to go over the sea for that.'

'I think,' said Orinoco, pushing up his goggles and shading his eyes against the gentle glow of the setting sun which was bathing everything in a soft orange colour, 'I think I can see the sea. It's just like Queen's Mere, only bigger.'

'A very great lot bigger,' said Bungo, joining his friend. They stood side by side, two small, rather bulky figures whose shadows grew longer and longer ahead of them on the grass. It really was an astonishing sight, all those miles and miles of water with here and there a little black dot

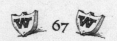

bobbing up and down on the waves.

'Imagine swimming in that,' said Orinoco at last.

'We wouldn't like it,' replied Bungo. 'It's got salt in it and that'd make all our fur stick together, and it's full of enormous fish.'

'I'm not afraid of fish.'

'You would be if you met a whale. It's about as big as one of those new lorries. I wonder what sea it is? Oh yes, here it is on the map. It's the North Sea.'

'It's not north, it's east,' argued Orinoco, turning to look at the sun which was setting behind them in the west and was now an enormous crimson ball just resting on the horizon.

'It's north of Wimbledon Common,' said Bungo patiently. 'That's why it's called the North Sea, I expect. Come on, we'd better find out if there's a good burrow round here. It'll be dark in a few minutes.'

The only burrows, however, belonged to rabbits and were too small for the Wombles, so they finally decided on a nice dry, sheltered patch at the bottom of a bank by some bushes. Orinoco, who

had a gift for making himself comfortable any-
where, made a thick mattress of dry ferns while
Bungo propped up the scooter and then covered it
with a piece of plastic sheeting. Then both of
them went looking for food and they soon discovered some tasty nettles and a really splendid piece
of fungus growing round the bottom of an old tree.
They already had a bag of dried buns which
Bungo's sharp eyes had spotted in a litter bin at a
garage when they had stopped for fuel earlier.
They lit a small campfire and Orinoco made a
stew in the saucepan which Madame Cholet had
provided, and Bungo toasted the buns and then
spread them with the last of the blackberry jam.

'This is the life,' said Orinoco contentedly. 'No
rules and regulations. No work. No exercises. I'm
really a Wandering Womble at heart.'

'Don't forget we're on a Special Secret Mission,'
said Bungo.

'Oh that,' said Orinoco, licking his whiskers to
get at the last of the jam. 'Oh *that*. Yes, of course.
Rather. Well, goodnight, old chap.' And he snug-
gled down into the heather with a satisfied smile
on his round face. Bungo stayed awake a little

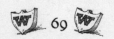

longer gazing up at the stars and then he too fell sound asleep.

It was some hours later that Bungo's instinct gave him a sudden warning. He was awake at once with his fur prickling and his ears back. For a moment he could hear nothing apart from Orinoco's snores and he was just beginning to think he must have had a bad dream when IT started again:

'*Chew-chew-chew-chump-chump-chump.*'

And it was getting nearer. Bungo dug Orinoco in the ribs and put his paw over his friend's mouth.

'Um, um, um,' said Orinoco, his eyes round with fright in the starlight.

'Listen,' whispered Bungo.

'*Chump-chump-chump*' went the sound and then there was a new noise, '*dingle-dingle-dingle*', like a bell, and at the same time out of the early morning mist there emerged a large, round, grey figure. Orinoco gave a squeak of fright and clutched Bungo for support. Bungo clutched back and they sat still as statues while the thing came right up to them. It stared at the two Wombles and then put back its head and said:

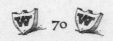

'*Maaaaaaaaaaa.*'

At once all the other chumping noises stopped and there was a whole chorus of '*Maaaaaaaaas*', all on different notes.

'Wh-wh-what is it?' whispered Orinoco.

'I d-d-don't know.'

The ring of ghostly figures grew closer until they formed a semicircle round the two Wombles. One of them got so near it put its foot on the handle of the saucepan and that stirred Bungo out of his fright and into action.

'Boo,' he said loudly, waving his arms, 'boo, boo, boo.'

There was a second's silence and then all the grey figures began to push and shove at each other as they tried to run away.

'Boo, BOO, BOO,' shouted Bungo, getting to his back paws.

The last of the grey shapes thudded away into the mist and Bungo, who was feeling braver by the second, ran after them waving his paws and shouting. Orinoco prudently stayed behind and got out one of the small booklets and flipped through the pages, and when Bungo returned looking very

pleased with himself Orinoco said, 'They were only sheep, you know. Nothing to be scared of at all. "Very gentle, stupid but useful animals", it says here.'

A remark which took all the wind out of Bungo just as neatly as Great Uncle Bulgaria would have done.

'How about breakfast?' suggested Orinoco. 'All this fresh air makes me feel quite peckish.'

They were on the road again by the time the sun came up, and as they chugged along Bungo

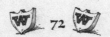

realised that in future they should be a little more careful where they camped. The sheep had been quite scaring enough, but supposing there had been cows or even a bull in that field! Bungo shivered violently, nearly unseating Orinoco who was dozing off on the back seat.

On and on and on they went so that all this new, exciting countryside through which they were passing became something of a blur, although they did stop for a short while to stare at the great mountainous ranges of the Lake District, taking it in turns with the binoculars to see who could find the tallest peak.

'It's very grand, isn't it?' Bungo said doubtfully.

'But not what I'd call snug,' agreed Orinoco. 'Tomsk'd like it, I expect. He could do some fast tobogganing down those slopes.'

There was an exciting moment after they had driven through Carlisle, for suddenly there was a sign welcoming them to Scotland.

'I don't care,' shouted Orinoco over his shoulder – he was driving at this point – 'I shall jolly well call it Abroad. After all it IS another country.'

Steep hills rose on either side of the road, but

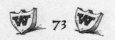

these were nothing compared with what was to come, for after Glasgow, ahead of them reared up the great Grampian Mountains.

Bungo suddenly pointed to a sign, nudged his friend in the ribs and then both Wombles burst into song.

'Ooooooo, I'll take the high road
And yooooo take the low road
And I'll be in Scotland before yoooooo . . .'

It wasn't exactly melodious, but it did a lot to raise their flagging spirits as they saw Loch Lomond come into view on their right.

'Oh my, oh my, oh my . . .' Bungo kept saying over and over to himself as he stared to left and then right at the mountains. He caught a glimpse of a red squirrel and then his bright little eyes spotted a whole line of red deer cantering grace-fully down a small valley, and the 'oh mys' became faster than ever.

They stopped for tea just past Fort William where they had taken on more fuel. It had been quite difficult to understand what the man at the garage had said, so they had had to point to what they wanted. And while he was pointing Orinoco had just happened to see a stall by the road where a woman was selling homemade cakes, so naturally they had bought a lovely-looking squashy chocolate sponge. It was a great deal more squashed by the time they got round to eating it, but nevertheless it vanished in double-quick time.

'I like foreign cooking,' said Orinoco.

'It isn't . . .' Bungo began and then stopped, because obviously Orinoco had made up his mind that this was going to be Abroad and that was that! So instead he said, 'Yes, so do I', and got out the map and the last of the sealed orders to make quite sure they knew where they were going.

'There was only one bit I didn't like much,' said Orinoco, tipping the last of the crumbs out of the paper bag down his throat, 'and that was Glencoe. It was sort of creepy. All my fur stood on end and although there was sunshine it felt cold somehow. I'm very sensitive in some ways, you know, Bungo. Pity we didn't get TWO cakes.'

'Um, um,' said Bungo. 'Look, Fort Augustus and then Loch Ness. I wonder why Great Uncle

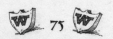

Bulgaria chose this bit for us to explore?' And he scratched his ears. The crash helmet made his fur itch.

'He was reading about it in *The Times*,' replied Orinoco, who was now licking the inside of the paper bag. 'I saw it on his desk one day when we reported for Exercises. I noticed it because he had drawn a red line underneath the name. It was all about something-or-other being found there – but I can't remember quite what it was now. You didn't know I could read words upside down, did you?'

'Oh, you can do everything, you can.'

'I didn't like the way you said that,' replied Orinoco, becoming alarmingly dignified.

'Hard luck,' said Bungo even more rudely.

A very young Womblish argument then took place full of 'and the same to you' and 'the same to you with knobs on' and 'the same to you with *brass* knobs on, so there!' which ended, of course, in a scuffle. Both of them felt much better for it, as there's nothing like a good fight between friends for getting rid of bad temper, and neither of them noticed that several pairs of eyes were watching them closely through the bushes.

The sun had vanished behind big black clouds which were scudding in from the west by the time that Loch Ness came into sight and a chill wind had sprung up. It ruffled the waters of the loch and sighed through the trees and made the branches shiver and shake.

'It's not a patch on Wimbledon Common,' said Bungo. What he really meant was that he found it all rather wild and frightening. 'Oh good, there's a telephone box. It must be nearly time to phone Tobermory.'

The idea of hearing that gruff voice cheered him up a great deal, and it took a lot of self-control not to go into the box and dial the number at once. But there was still half an hour to wait, so they scrambled down the bank to the edge of the loch and played ducks and drakes with all the flat stones they could find.

'I wonder if there are whales in it,' said Orinoco. 'It's almost as big as a sea after all.'

'I don't think so. Come on, it's twenty-five past six.'

Bungo's paws were fairly shaking with excitement as he dialled the number, and then there

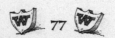

was a *poop-poop-poop* sound and he put in the right money and the pooping stopped and Tobermory said right in his ear, 'Well, young Womble?'

'We're here,' said Bungo shakily.

'Of course you're there. But where *is* there? Try not to be more of a fool than you can help,' said Tobermory at his gruffest, for he understood very well how Bungo was feeling and had himself been pacing up and down by the telephone box for the last twenty minutes waiting for the call. He had, with his usual foresight, hung a notice on the door saying OUT OF ORDER to stop anyone else using it during this period.

'Loch, Loch Ness. SD 4 and 5 reporting to SD 2. OWW.'

'Lot of rigmarole,' muttered Tobermory. 'Message received and understood. Is everything all right?'

'Yes, thank you. How – how is everyone?'

There was the slightest pause before Tobermory replied briskly, 'Mustn't grumble. Place seems almost peaceful without you two. What's it like up there?'

'It's very wild,' said Bungo slowly, 'and there

seem to be more wild animals than there are Human Beings. We've seen red squirrels and red deer . . .'

'And sheep,' said Orinoco, who was breathing down Bungo's neck.

'I can't see much at the moment,' Bungo went on. 'It's got very dark suddenly. Oh!'

'What is it? Speak up, young Womble.'

'I thought I saw something moving round the back of this box . . .' said Bungo, breathing on the glass and at once misting it up.

'Report tomorrow at 18.00 hours and don't go getting fanciful. Red deer won't eat you. They're vegetarians like we are. The OC sends his regards and . . .'

Poop, poop, poop, went the telephone and at the same moment the door of the telephone box was opened from the outside and, before either Bungo or Orinoco realised what was happening, something soft and heavy was thrown over their heads and a voice said, 'Got 'em.'

CHAPTER 6

Great Uncle Bulgaria's Great Idea

Tobermory left the telephone box and removed the OUT OF ORDER notice and made his way slowly back to the burrow. Two things were weighing on his mind. The first was that he thought he had heard real fright in Bungo's voice when he had said 'Oh!' like that, and the second was that things were far from being well at the burrow, for shortly after Bungo and Orinoco had left on the Great

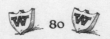

Adventure what must have been an extra large lorry had thundered across the Common.

Tobermory, who had been about to enter his Workshop at the time, felt the whole place shudder and suddenly to his dismay he saw a large crack zigzag across the ceiling. A fine white dust fell on his grey fur and made him sneeze violently.

'Bless you,' said Great Uncle Bulgaria from the doorway.

'Thank you.' Tobermory blew his nose and then pointed at the crack. 'It won't give way completely,' he said. 'The whole place is too strongly reinforced for that, but it's not nice. It's not nice at all. Think I'll have a look outside.'

'Take Wellington with you,' said Great Uncle Bulgaria. 'He could do with a breath of fresh air.'

'He's a good young Womble,' said Tobermory, which made Wellington, who was standing out in the passage, shuffle his paws with embarrassment.

They went to see what had caused the crack and what they discovered made Tobermory draw in his breath sharply. There had definitely been a slight landslide.

'Bless my boots!' said Tobermory.

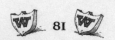

'Is it bad?' Wellington asked anxiously.

'Not bad exactly, but not good either. Ho-hum.'
Tobermory walked round the piece of earth
which had moved, shaking his grey head. That
this sort of thing should happen on his Wimbledon
Common was most unsettling in more ways than
one. He looked across the grass with his back to
the road, thinking deeply. For some time now he
had had an idea at the back of his mind, but it
needed a great deal more thought before he said
anything; so he only got out his tape measure and
gave one end to Wellington and then went off,
unrolling it behind him and making notes in the
small book he always kept in his apron pocket.

Later, as he walked back to the burrow for his
evening meal, he shook his head again. As soon as
supper was over and he had made his report to the
oldest Womble he said gravely, 'We may have to
act faster than we planned.'

'Oh?'

'Yes. When we strengthened the burrow after
the Awful Rainstorms that time we only believed
we had *natural* dangers to deal with. No amount of
rain or depth of snow could cause us any harm as

we are, but this shaking up of the ground by Human Beings is something quite different. Not to put too fine a point on it, we're sinking.'

'Sinking!' repeated Great Uncle Bulgaria, putting on both pairs of spectacles.

'Sinking. I feared as much when I first started taking measurements. Now I'm certain. We're down a further two inches since yesterday in some parts.'

There was a long silence while the two old friends looked steadily at each other. Up till now Great Uncle Bulgaria had secretly rather enjoyed the whole business of Operation Wandering Womble. It had been a little like a splendid game, but now it had become suddenly serious and a little shiver of alarm went through his white fur. He was, after all, responsible for all the Wombles of Wimbledon Common.

'How long can we last?' he asked in a low voice.

'Difficult to say. The burrow itself is strong enough; it's the earth round it which is giving way. If all this ridiculous traffic has done this to us, I can't imagine what it must be doing to the homes of the Human Beings,' said Tobermory with a snort. 'Silly creatures that they are, they probably won't realise the danger until one of their houses falls down. Serve them right too.'

'Quite. Can't you give me any idea how soon we may be forced to leave?'

'It could be a year, or two years. Or it could be tomorrow. All I can say is, we must find a new home and the sooner the better. Unless . . .'

'Well?'

'I've been looking through some of our old records and there is an early Womble burrow right in the middle of the Common. It's deep, very deep, but there's one drawback unfortunately. It's small. We should be very overcrowded and you know how long it takes to enlarge a burrow, because of the difficulty of getting rid of all the earth one has to dig up. But in an emergency . . .'

'Ho-hum.'

Great Uncle Bulgaria shot his friend a shrewd look and then went over to the map and stared at it with a wrinkled forehead.

'Thank you for being so honest,' he said. 'It's always better to know the full truth.' It was lucky that he was not looking at Tobermory as he spoke, as that Womble for some strange reason seemed oddly upset by these words. 'Very well, we shall have to fall back on our reserves, the Second Scouting Party.'

'They're not trained.'

'If the situation is as desperate as you say, they will have to go out scouting untrained.'

'Where to?'

'That's a point. It can't be another long journey such as Bungo and Orinoco have made. We must look for somewhere nearer home. Leave it to me, old friend. Just ask SD 3 and 6 to report to me at 08.00 hours.'

'Eight o'clock tomorrow morning,' said Tobermory. 'Very well. It may not be as bad as I've made out.' But he didn't sound very sure of his own words and once Great Uncle Bulgaria was on his own, he shuffled back to his desk looking very old and frail indeed. He knew all about dangers and his fur had that faint prickly feel about it, which told him very plainly that his Wombles were in peril. He sat for a long while staring at the ceiling until, because he was very tired, he almost felt that he could see it bulging more and more.

'Nonsense!' he said sharply to himself. 'This is no time for being fanciful, Bulgaria. Pull yourself together, Womble. Somewhere nearer home, but where? Where?'

He picked up yesterday's edition of *The Times* to try and calm himself. Nothing but troubles everywhere in the world as far as he could see. Slowly he turned the pages until he came to the centre of the paper. Ah, that was better. The Court Circular. Nothing unsettling in that, he was sure, and then suddenly he stiffened and read the words again, and a quite astonishing idea came into his mind.

'Well,' said Great Uncle Bulgaria to the silent Operations Room, 'well – why not? It's worth a try anyway. Ho-hum.'

And he dropped the newspaper and rubbed his white paws together, chuckling to himself.

When Tobermory heard Great Uncle Bulgaria's plan the following morning he was so startled that he could only stare with his mouth wide open and his grey fur standing up on end.

'Send them scouting *where?*' he croaked at last.

'If it's good enough for Her,' said Great Uncle Bulgaria, who was having a hard struggle not to burst out laughing, 'then surely it's good enough for Us? Ah, I think I hear SD 3 and 6 outside. Come to think of it, you can usually hear SD 6 nearly everywhere. Open the door for them, would you?'

Standing outside were Wellington and Tomsk.

'He said I was to come,' said Tomsk in a hoarse whisper. 'He said you'd given him a message to give me, Tobermory. I told him it said SECRET and KEEP OUT, but he said . . .'

'He said, you said, I said,' snapped Tobermory. 'Come in and stop chattering, do.' Tomsk looked hurt but did as he was told, with Wellington at his heels. Wellington appeared far less tired than he had done for weeks as he'd had a good night's sleep. In fact, as he no longer had a watch, he had slept right through breakfast and had had to snatch a sandwich off the trolley. He was still chewing now.

'Oh my,' said Tomsk who had, of course, never seen the Operations Room since all the maps had been put up. 'Oh my, oh my, oh MY!'

'Yes, yes, I dare say,' said Great Uncle Bulgaria, who was longing to put his second plan into motion. 'Now then, you two, you're going to be our Second Scouting Party. From now on you will be referred to as SD – Special Duties – 3 and 6.'

'Oh!' Wellington's face lit up with pleasure and excitement.

Tomsk, who didn't really understand what the old Womble meant, kept quiet. He had long ago discovered that it was the best thing to do in difficult situations.

'Wellington will explain it all to you later,' said Great Uncle Bulgaria, who understood perfectly what was happening in Tomsk's slow brain. 'Well, Wellington?'

'I-I-I,' stuttered Wellington, whose head was going round and round at this unexpected news. He had tried to imagine sometimes how splendid he would feel if he should ever be chosen as a scout, but he had never dreamed his wish would come true. He wasn't brave and dashing like Bungo, or strong like Tomsk, or sure of himself like Orinoco. He was just Wellington, who hadn't got very good eyesight – for a Womble – and who got lost even on the Common because of his terrible habit of daydreaming.

'Stop daydreaming,' said Great Uncle Bulgaria, who understood Wellington's brain very well too.

'S-Sir,' said Wellington, clicking his back paws together and standing stiff as a ramrod. He rather spoilt the whole effect by smiling so widely that his eyes practically vanished.

'Good.' Great Uncle Bulgaria nodded. 'Thought you'd be pleased. You deserve the job, Wellington; you've worked extremely hard during these last few weeks. These last dark weeks during which we have all had . . .'

'Ah-HEM,' said Tobermory, who could always tell when Great Uncle Bulgaria was going to start making a speech, and who was in no mood for one himself this morning.

'Yes. Well, as you know, Bungo and Orinoco are now out looking for a new Home for us,' and Great Uncle Bulgaria pointed at the map where two of the red-topped drawing pins were now stuck side by side on the banks of Loch Ness. 'However, we've now decided, as time's getting a bit short, that we may have to look for somewhere closer to the Common.'

'*Much* closer,' said Tobermory drily.

'We can't spare the pair of you a week in which to train,' went on Great Uncle Bulgaria, ignoring this remark, 'so Tobermory will give you a Crash Course.'

'Crash?' said Tomsk, desperately trying to follow all this.

'Quick,' snapped Great Uncle Bulgaria. 'Just today in other words. You're fit enough, Tomsk, and, Wellington, you're clever enough. You'll have to help each other. I've drawn up a list of things I want done and first of all you, Tomsk, are going to have a fitting.'

Tomsk stared at the old Womble dumbly. He was lost again.

'A fitting for some very special clothes,' said Great Uncle Bulgaria patiently. 'I've written it all down here. Take this paper along to Miss Adelaide and then do as she tells you. Wellington, I want you to study this map of the Underground and then go to the Workshop for supplies. Tobermory, here are copies of these orders for you. At 12.00 hours every-

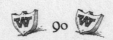

body is to report back to me. Is that clear?'

'Um,' said Tomsk.

'Yes,' said Wellington breathlessly. He still hadn't taken it in properly that he was going to be a scout.

'Fairly,' said Tobermory, glancing through his orders.

'Dismiss, all except SD 3,' ordered Great Uncle Bulgaria.

Tobermory prodded the still bemused Tomsk out of the room, and Wellington moved over to the desk where Great Uncle Bulgaria was spreading out the map of the London Underground.

'There is just one thing,' Wellington said timidly.

'Um.' Great Uncle Bulgaria glanced up.

'Where are we going?' Wellington asked.

'Shouldn't really tell you that. You should have sealed orders like Bungo and Orinoco, but seeing that this is an emergency situation I may as well tell you now,' replied Great Uncle Bulgaria, who was, in fact, simply longing to disclose his plan. He took a deep breath and gazed up at Wellington's hopeful face.

'You,' said Great Uncle Bulgaria, prodding the young Womble with his stick, 'you are going to have the great, the very great honour of exploring a very *special* place.' He paused.

Wellington's eyes were now as round as his spectacles. A lorry thundered along the new road, but neither of them noticed it for once.

'You,' said Great Uncle Bulgaria, rising stiffly to his feet and removing the cap with the red trimming and tucking it smartly under his arm, 'are going to explore the gardens of Her Most Gracious Majesty at Buckingham Palace. Well, young Womble, what have you to say to *that*?'

CHAPTER 7

Tomsk and Wellington Set Out

Although Great Uncle Bulgaria was a very wise old Womble with a great deal of general knowledge at his pawtips, there were one or two points on which he was a trifle shaky – as poor Tomsk was to discover. However, all this was still in the future and, for the moment, there was so much to be done that even Tobermory forgot to do any more measuring as he hurried from one part of the

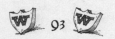

burrow to the other, muttering to himself and making notes in his little book. It was not until nearly teatime that he managed to have a few minutes to think things over, when he joined Miss Adelaide and Madame Cholet who were both busy in one of the Workshops. They too had now signed the Wombles' Official Secrets Act and were now SD 7 and SD 8.

'I don't know,' he said, sitting down rather heavily as he suddenly realised how tired he was. 'It's a mad plan. It'll never work.'

'It might,' said Miss Adelaide, who was working away at a somewhat strange sewing machine that Tobermory had made up from spare bits and pieces some years ago. The main wheel had come from a baby's pram and the handle had once been a car crank; but it worked very well as did all Tobermory's inventions. As he looked at it now he forgot all his worries for a moment, and went over and got down a can of beech-nut oil and squeezed a few drops on the machine while Miss Adelaide watched him. Both she and Madame Cholet had, of course, been given all the latest OWW news, but whatever they thought of it they kept to themselves.

'There, that's better, it was getting a bit squeaky,' said Tobermory, putting the can away in exactly the right place on the shelf. 'Apart from anything else there's our work here piling up. I haven't managed to get near the main Workshop all day. Goodness knows what kind of mess it will be in by now.'

'No, it won't,' contradicted Madame Cholet with a wheezy chuckle – she was stout, even by Womble standards. 'Miss Adelaide has put Form Two to work there, so all is well.'

'Young Wombles in *my* Workshop!' said Tobermory, rather annoyed.

'Certainly. It's good practical experience for them,' replied Miss Adelaide calmly. 'I've told them to sort everything properly and they will!'

'What you need, Tobermory,' said Madame Cholet, putting down her sewing which looked like a big black fur cat, 'is a nice hot drink. I'll fetch you some nettle tea from the kitchen.'

'It won't work, you know,' said Tobermory gloomily as Madame Cholet left. 'It can't. The gardens are probably full of soldiers with guns and goodness knows what else.'

'We shall see,' replied Miss Adelaide, snipping off a piece of scarlet thread and shaking out the coat on which she was working. 'When do Tomsk and Wellington set out?'

'22.00 hours, that's ten o'clock tonight. They'll get caught, you'll see. And locked up and questioned and then the newspapers'll get hold of it and there'll be a big Womble hunt. It'll be the finish of us all.'

'Nonsense,' said Miss Adelaide in the kind of voice she normally used when speaking to very small Wombles, which was not at all the kind of voice that Tobermory (who was second only to Great Uncle Bulgaria) was used to. His fur rose, but Miss Adelaide took no notice of this at all and began to work on a pair of black trousers as she went on. 'Nonsense and you know it. We Wombles are a far older race of creatures than Human Beings and they have never yet taken any notice of us. Their children do, of course, from time to time and I have often thought that in many ways they are far more clever than the grown-ups. They see us, they even talk to us, but they normally have the good sense to keep this to themselves.'

'But . . .' began Tobermory.

'Excuse *me*,' said Miss Adelaide in a way which had made many a young Womble shake in his fur. 'Excuse *me*, but I had not quite finished what I wished to say.'

'Sorry,' mumbled Tobermory, who was starting to feel that he was once again in the back row of the Womblegarten.

'Thank you. As I was about to say, I always considered Wellington one of my brightest pupils and I am confident that he will be able to deal with any situation which may arise.' And, *snip*, she cut off another piece of cotton.

Tobermory waited for several seconds until he was sure that this time Miss Adelaide really *had* finished speaking and then he said, 'But Tomsk isn't like Wellington.'

'No. I agree. However, he will have Wellington to look after him and,' Miss Adelaide smiled faintly, 'and he will also have further protection.' And she neatly folded away the black trousers as Madame Cholet came in with a tea tray.

'All the same,' said Tobermory some while later, 'all the same and whatever *does* happen, I wish we didn't have to leave the Common. There is that other burrow after all . . . Oh well.' He got stiffly to his feet and glanced at his watch. 'Time for the telephone call,' he said and went off with his shoulders bowed.

'He seems to feel it more than any of us,' said Madame Cholet sadly. She had a very soft heart and hated to see any Womble looking unhappy.

'Yes,' Miss Adelaide nodded. 'He is deeply attached to the Common. It is a great shame. May I see that coloured drawing again, please.'

Madame Cholet passed over the picture which had come from a child's school book and Miss Adelaide held it at arm's length and looked from it to the clothes on which the pair of them had been so busy. A faint look of doubt crossed her face and then she stiffened her shoulders.

'Nonsense,' she said to herself. 'Of course they'll be all right.'

Wellington and Tomsk themselves were in far too much of a whirl of excitement to have the time to feel scared. They had been pushed from place to place by Tobermory, they had been measured and turned round and round like tops by

Miss Adelaide and Madame Cholet. They had been given a whole list of orders by Great Uncle Bulgaria and, when at last they crept to bed early, Tomsk whispered, 'I know why it's called a Crash Course. It's because you feel as though you have been in a crash. Like that time I went skiing and bumped into the snow Womble.'

'Shh,' implored Wellington, whose own head was spinning. 'I'll never remember, oh, I know I won't.' And he put his paws over his ears and shut his eyes tight as he tried to recall all his instructions. Luckily for both of them Wellington did have a very clear brain, and some time during the evening everything seemed to click neatly into place and he fell deeply asleep and snored almost as loudly as Tomsk.

However, it seemed as if they had hardly been asleep at all when Madame Cholet called them and led them, blinking and yawning, to the kitchen, where she had prepared a meal which was a mixture of breakfast and supper. Wombles can, naturally, eat at any time and in nearly any circumstances, and the food soon vanished at high speed while Madame Cholet watched them fondly.

'And a little something to keep up your strength,' she said, handing them a small picnic box very similar to the one she had prepared for Bungo and Orinoco. There was never any shortage of boxes on the Common.

'I'd better carry it,' replied Wellington. 'You're not supposed to carry anything except your wooden rifle. Remember?'

The Wombles do not approve of weapons and, although a few toy guns had been found over the years, they were always kept well locked away. Tobermory, after carefully studying the coloured picture, had picked out the toy rifle which looked most like the one in the drawing and had cleaned, oiled and polished it. He was waiting with it in the Workshop when the two young Wombles arrived. He looked extremely worried, but nobody really noticed this for they were too busy dealing with Wellington and Tomsk. Great Uncle Bulgaria and Miss Adelaide were the calmest of the group as they stood side by side watching what was happening.

First Wellington was helped into a pair of dark blue workman's overalls and a dark blue cap. Then

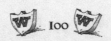

he was given a toolbag to sling over one shoulder, next some pieces of wood that had been nailed together so that they could be unfolded to make a kind of small fence and finally a red lantern with WBC painted on it in white.

'Wimbledon Borough Council,' said Tobermory regretfully. 'I didn't have time to find out what the letters should be for where you're going. I'm sorry about that.' He hated not getting everything exactly right.

'You've done an excellent job, Tobermory,' said Great Uncle Bulgaria. 'Quite amazing, all things considered. Now, Tomsk,' and he rubbed his white paws together.

Tomsk's outfit was quite different and a great deal more colourful and splendid. First there were the trousers and then a pair of boots that were so highly polished that Tomsk could see his own round, surprised face in them. Next came the scarlet jacket with the equally shiny gold buttons. The jacket fitted him exactly, which explained all the careful measuring that had been done on his large form. In fact it fitted him so well that Tomsk hardly dared to breathe in case all the buttons popped off the front, so he stood very still with his shoulders well back and his eyes fixed on the opposite wall.

Last, but not least, Madame Cholet climbed on a chair and with very great care lowered the black, furry, tall thing on to Tomsk's head and slid the chinstrap just under his quivering nose. He could hardly see anything now because the black fur stuff was right in front of his eyes. Every time he breathed in and out it went up and down and made him want to sneeze.

'Shouldn't that strap be under my chin, please?' whispered Tomsk, trying to squint sideways.

'Not in the picture, it isn't,' said Madame Cholet. 'You'll soon get used to it.'

'The rifle,' said Tobermory, taking it over very carefully indeed. 'Treat it gently, Tomsk. Very, very gently. As if it were a – a . . .'

'Golf club?' suggested Tomsk, who loved playing golf just as much as Orinoco loved eating.

'Yes.'

'Well?' asked Miss Adelaide.

Great Uncle Bulgaria, Tobermory, Madame Cholet and Wellington all gazed at the motionless

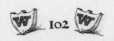

Tomsk. They walked round him, they shook their heads, they went '*tsk, tsk, tsk*' and 'ho-hum' while he watched them from out of the corners of his eyes. All he could see was their back paws circling the floor.

'Astonishing,' said Great Uncle Bulgaria at last.

'Not bad,' said Tobermory.

'Marvellous,' said Madame Cholet.

'Oh my, oh my, oh MY!' said Wellington.

Tomsk really did strike a magnificent figure as he stood there. He had always been a fine-looking

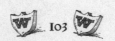

Womble and now, dressed as a Grenadier Guardsman, he was indeed splendid to behold.

'He even frightens *me* a little,' whispered Great Uncle Bulgaria behind one white paw to Tobermory. Tobermory grunted and then glanced at his watch.

'Yes, yes,' Great Uncle Bulgaria agreed. 'Time to be off. I'll come and see you go.'

They filed out of the Workshop and down the passage, with Tomsk having to bend at the knees to prevent his splendid black fur hat brushing the ceilings. Tobermory opened the great door – normally only used when they went on their Midsummer outing in the Silver Grey Womble, which was a mixture between a very large car and a small coach. Wellington and Tomsk climbed into the back of this magnificent conveyance, and Tobermory got into the front, putting on the cap that he always kept in the side pocket together with a map of London. Madame Cholet handed up the picnic box, which had almost been forgotten in the excitement, and Great Uncle Bulgaria saluted smartly as WOM I purred softly into life. Tomsk saluted back, looking straight ahead as he did so. It was a very stirring moment and even Miss Adelaide gave a slight sniff, which was most unlike her.

It was very dark out on the Common, but that didn't bother Tobermory, who still had excellent sight for his age. He even managed to make out the figure of one small, rather lonely-looking Womble who was hanging about at a certain place, slapping his paws to keep warm. This Womble waved at WOM 1 and also shook his head. Tobermory sighed deeply, but said nothing and returned the salute.

'One worry at a time,' he told himself sternly. 'So Bungo and Orinoco haven't telephoned yet which makes them,' he looked at the small clock which glowed on the dashboard, 'which makes them five hours late. Silly young creatures, what *can* have happened to them? No, they *must* be all right. Bungo can talk his way out of anything!'

And with that cheering thought Tobermory turned the car off the track which led across the Common and into the main road and set course for Buckingham Palace.

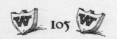

CHAPTER 8

The MacWomble

As it happened, Bungo and Orinoco were very far from all right. Ever since they had been captured in the telephone box they had been prisoners, but why they had been captured or by whom they still had not the faintest idea. They had fought as best they could, but the sacking which had been thrown over their heads had hampered them and also the enemy had been greater in number. They had been

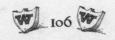

bundled outside, none too gently, their paws tied behind them and then, still covered in sacking, they had been marched for what seemed like miles and miles. Both of them had been, and were, extremely frightened, but they hadn't said so until much later that evening when they were alone.

'Where are we?' whispered Orinoco.

'How should I know?' replied Bungo.

They had been tied up back to back and their own scarves had replaced the sacking. But if they could not see, they could still sniff and touch and, in the case of Orinoco, feel the pangs of really severe hunger.

Sniff, sniff, sniff, went Bungo, turning his head from side to side.

'It's a burrow of sorts,' he said in a low voice, 'but a very primitive sort of burrow. It smells of damp earth.'

'It's a stone floor,' replied Orinoco. 'I can feel it through my fur. Tobermory wouldn't think much of it. Oh I do wish . . .' His voice rose slightly.

'Don't,' said Bungo sternly. 'I wish it too, but it's no good just wishing. We must *do* something. Wriggle.'

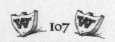

'Why?'

'We might get this string a bit looser.'

They wriggled and twisted and jumped up and down, but whoever had tied them up had done it very well.

'What's that?' said Bungo suddenly, pausing in mid-wriggle.

'My stomach,' replied Orinoco sadly.

'No, no, apart from that. Someone's coming. Brace up, young Womble.'

There was a *clump, clump, clump* outside and voices, and then the sound of a chain rattling and a key turning in the lock.

'Oooooooo,' said Orinoco.

'Nothing could be more frightening than Great Uncle Bulgaria when he's really cross with you – think of that,' whispered Bungo, whose own fur was standing just as stiffly on end as Orinoco's.

The door swung open and a gust of cold, damp air swept through the cell as a gruff voice said, 'Up with the pair of you.'

It was very difficult getting to their back paws when they were so trussed up, but they managed

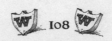

it somehow and then the voice went on, 'I'm to untie you, that's what Himself says.'

'Himself?' asked Bungo, who thought this was a funny way to talk.

'Aye. None of your English tricks now or it'll be the worse for you.'

It was at least something to have their paws free, and the two young Wombles rubbed their wrists and flipped them up and down while they were being marched out of the cell and down the draughty corridor. The ground felt rough and uneven under their paws, but when they were pushed up a short flight of stone steps and into another passage it grew smoother, and Bungo guessed that they were being taken to a more important part of the burrow and not, as he had secretly feared, to an even nastier cell. Another door was opened and both Wombles could sense that they were now in a much larger room with a great many other creatures in it. There was a lot of soft whispering which died down into silence so that they could hear the sound of their own paw-steps on the stone floor and, in Orinoco's case, the uneasy rumbling of his insides.

'Stop,' commanded the voice. 'Yon's the prisoners.'

'So I can see,' came a sharp reply in a tone which, for some strange reason, made Bungo think of Great Uncle Bulgaria. 'Take off those scarves.'

The scarves were unknotted and pulled away and Bungo and Orinoco found themselves blinking in astonishment at the scene before them. They were in a very large room indeed, with thick wooden rafters criss-crossing the ceiling and with rough-looking walls that had what appeared to be tattered pieces of material pinned to them. There were some long wooden tables and benches, and in front of them a kind of platform on which was set a big wooden chair with a high carved back and carved arms. It was the occupant of this throne-like chair who made their eyes bulge in their heads.

It was a large, extremely fierce-looking Womble.

'Oh my,' whispered Orinoco.

'H-hallo,' said Bungo hesitantly.

'You'll speak when you're spoken to and not before,' said the Womble, folding his arms and scowling more than ever. His fur was just starting to turn grey and he was wearing a strange sort of

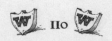

little cap on his head and a skirt, the pattern of which was vaguely familiar.

'Do you know who I am?' rapped out the Womble.

Bungo and Orinoco shook their heads. A soft murmur of surprise ran round the hall and was instantly stilled as the grey Womble glared about him.

'I'm Cairngorm Womble. Or, as they call me in the Highlands, the MacWomble the Terrible.'

Orinoco was about to whisper 'oh my' again, but luckily Bungo dug him in the ribs just in time to stop him.

The MacWomble rose from his chair as he spoke and slowly climbed down from the platform and came up to Bungo and Orinoco, who were still too surprised to know whether they were relieved or frightened to have been taken prisoner by another family of Wombles. The MacWomble was certainly fierce enough to scare anybody.

'I know who you are,' he said, staring at them with narrowed eyes. 'You're spies from Abroad.'

A word which made Orinoco shoot a pleased 'I told you so' look at Bungo.

'Wipe that grin off your face,' roared the MacWomble and Orinoco did. Instantly.

'I thought as much,' said the MacWomble, clasping his paws behind him and slowly walking round his shivering prisoners. 'You've come from England as spies, have you not?'

Bungo and Orinoco shook their heads violently.

'Oh yes, yer have,' contradicted the MacWomble very softly in Bungo's ear. Bungo glanced at him out of the corners of his eyes, swallowed and then looked straight ahead. 'You've come to discover our Great Secret. That's it, isn't it?' the MacWomble went on softly.

'N-n-n-no,' said Bungo.

'Ah-HA,' said the MacWomble. 'Well, time will tell. We'll find out about that, don't make any mistake. My clansmen have been following you ever since you crossed the border on your wee scooter.'

'Have they?' said Bungo with interest. 'We didn't notice them.'

'Aye, you wouldn't have. You two are about as observant as a pair of Human Beings. You dinna deserve the name Womble.'

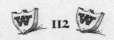

A remark which there and then made Bungo forget all about being frightened and quite determined to somehow prove the MacWomble wrong.

'Well, we jolly well are Wombles, from London too, so there!' said Bungo loudly.

There was a moment's silence and then the MacWomble stopped pacing round and round the pair of them, and said in a not quite so fierce voice, 'Ah-HA. Well, we'll see. If Wombles you are, then you shall be treated right. Never let it be said that we of the Highlands were short on courtesy.'

'Now he tells us,' Bungo said out of the corner of his mouth, but Orinoco's sharp nose had caught a whiff, a very definite whiff, of delicious food and he was no longer listening to the conversation.

'You'll sit with me at the high table,' said the MacWomble, 'where I can keep an eye on you,' and he clapped his paws together. At this a truly terrible noise started. It was far more upsetting than anything that had happened so far and Bungo and Orinoco fairly bristled. The noise rose and fell in a series of howls and hoots and moans. It grew louder and louder and then the doors were thrown open and in marched slowly two small Wombles blowing into weird-looking instruments, their cheeks all puffed up with effort.

Groan, groan, moan, moan, yell, went the things they were playing.

'The pipes,' said the MacWomble above the awful din. 'You'll no have them where you come from, I'm thinking.'

Bungo and Orinoco exchanged glances which said quite plainly, 'No, we *don't*, thank goodness . . .'

Fortunately the MacWomble didn't notice and led them to two places that were hastily being laid at one of the tables. Bungo found it very difficult to concentrate with this dreadful noise going on, but nothing would have kept Orinoco from his food, and he managed to eat so much that even the MacWomble was impressed and said, 'My, you're a grand one for your food.'

'Very nice it is too,' said Orinoco, taking a fourth helping.

In spite of the bagpipe players marching up and down Bungo also managed to do quite well, and by the finish he was starting to feel more hopeful about the future. He wasn't stupid and he had a kind of an idea that the MacWomble might not be

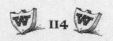

quite as terrible as he pretended. Also two things puzzled him. First and most important, what was the Great Secret, and second, why was the skirt thing so like something else he knew?

'Well, are you going to enjoy staying here as our guests?' asked the MacWomble, cracking nuts in his large paws in a manner which earned him Orinoco's deepest respect. He had had to use his teeth.

'Very much, I'm sure,' Bungo said politely. 'But we can't stay for long, you know. We shall have to get home to report.'

'Och, will you now? And if you should do that what would happen? Why, we'd be invaded again. No, thank you. Here you are and here you'll stay,' said the MacWomble firmly. Like Tomsk, Bungo had learnt that there are times when it is better to keep quiet, so somehow he managed to hold his tongue. But of one thing he was quite, quite determined. He and Orinoco were going to escape! Obviously it was no good all the Wimbledon Wombles travelling up to Loch Ness as it was already inhabited (although what the Highland Wombles had to do in the way of work was a mystery), so the sooner he and Orinoco returned to Wimbledon and reported the failure of their mission, the better.

'I'm glad to see that you're learning sense,' said the MacWomble. He clapped his paws again and the tables were pulled back against the walls and a space cleared in the middle of the hall. Another clap and two young Wombles moved out into the middle and stood with their paws on their waists. Yet again the strange music of the bagpipes started up and the two Wombles began to dance, first with one paw up above their heads and then the other as they jigged round and round. It seemed to be a very exhausting dance, but also extremely popular and all the other Wombles in the hall clapped their paws in time to it.

'Och, that's a bonny Highland fling they do,' said the MacWomble. 'Do you not think so?'

'Very – er – bonny,' agreed Bungo, who was glad he hadn't got to do it.

'It keeps us warm of a winter's evening,' went on the MacWomble. 'We get a rare lot of snow here, you ken, and it gets mighty cold.'

'Did you build this burrow?' asked Bungo. The hall was certainly far bigger than any of the rooms

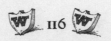

back at Wimbledon, even the Playroom where the Wombles and Ladders game was.

'Part of it, part of it. This bit's a cave inside the loch and very useful it is too. That is –' The MacWomble suddenly seemed to change his mind about what he had been going to say. 'That is, we like it fine. Time for bed.'

Bungo and Orinoco were pleased to find that they were not being returned to their cell, but to a room where there was plenty of straw on the floor and a high, very small window. All the same the door was locked behind them, a fact which reminded them that in spite of the good supper, they were still thought of as prisoners.

'Not a bad sort of meal,' said Orinoco, gently rubbing his stomach. 'Could have done with more of it though.'

'Don't you ever think of anything but food?' Bungo asked crossly.

'Not often.'

'You realise, of course, that we haven't rung Tobermory and that he'll be getting worried?'

'Perhaps he'll come and find us,' said Orinoco hopefully.

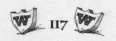

'Ha!' said Bungo. 'He doesn't even know where we are. We'll have to escape somehow. We can't stay here for ever and ever and, besides, I want to know what this Secret is, don't you?'

'Um,' replied Orinoco, who was more than half asleep. Bungo went across and shook him.

'Come on,' he said, 'let's try that window.'

'Too high,' replied Orinoco, yawning and scratching.

'Not if I stand on your shoulders. Do *try* and help.'

Bungo pushed and shoved his sleepy friend across the room and up against the wall. Orinoco braced himself and Bungo took a leap and somehow, scrambling and scrabbling, managed to get on his shoulders.

'Just goes to show,' he said breathlessly as he clung to a stone that jutted out from the wall, 'that Tobermory was right to make us take all that exercise. Oh, do stand still.'

'Doing my best,' grumbled Orinoco, whose nose was being pressed into the side of the cave.

'It's jolly stiff,' wheezed Bungo, who was struggling with the window which had probably never

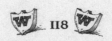

been opened before. In the end he had to put his elbow through the glass which made, it seemed to him, a horribly loud tinkling noise as it fell out.

'I think I can just about – squeeze – through,' puffed Bungo, half in and half out, his back paws kicking. Orinoco, relieved of his friend's weight, looked upwards and said, 'What can you see?'

'Water,' Bungo replied in a whisper. 'Lots and lots of water. We must be right beside Loch Ness.'

'I say,' said Orinoco, straightening up and suddenly forgetting how pleasantly tired and full he was, 'I say, old chap, I've just remembered something. Do you recall how I told you there was something else in that *Times* which I'd forgotten? Well, it all comes back to me and it was all about . . .'

'Shut up for a minute,' interrupted Bungo who was now about three-quarters of the way out of the window. He was nicely protected from the jagged bits of glass by his overalls. 'I believe I can see something out in the loch. It's a very funny shape, all odd bumps and lumps and it's swimming ever so fast. I wonder what it can be?'

'Look here, I say, Bungo, Bungo,' said Orinoco,

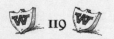

jumping up and down and trying to grasp the back paws of his friend. 'Bungo, old chap, don't, don't . . .'

'Can't help myself,' replied Bungo, who had ventured just that little bit too far in his anxiety to have a closer look at the strange creature swimming in the water below. 'What's the matter anyway – oh – *whoo-ps* . . .'

There was a moment's silence and then a splash as Bungo, his paws thrashing, overbalanced and tumbled head first into the cold, starlit waters below.

'Just remembered,' said Orinoco, slowly buckling at the knees and sinking gracefully to the ground, 'just remembered what I read, old thing. There's a monster in that loch. A dreadful, awful, terrible monster . . .'

There was no reply from outside except the gentle splash of the waters of Loch Ness against the shore.

CHAPTER 9

Nessie

It was at the actual moment that Bungo overtoppled and plunged head first towards the cold, grey waters of Loch Ness that another side of Tobermory's training proved its worth. Bungo, scarcely without thinking, straightened out and neatly entered the loch in a perfect dive. It caused hardly a ripple and, even as he went down and down, he couldn't help feeling pleased with himself.

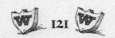

However, as he continued to go down and down at quite an alarming rate, he soon stopped being pleased and pushed his clasped front paws upwards towards the surface. Slowly, slowly, he began to rise, but his overalls were by now very heavy with water they had absorbed and they stopped him going up as fast as he should have done. The result was that by the time Bungo reached the surface again, he was gasping for breath and all he could do was to float with his chest going up and down like a pair of bellows.

'Goodness, oh dear, oh my,' gasped Bungo, flat on his back and staring up at the night sky. 'Oh, it is deep. Oh dear. I can see stars.'

Which was hardly surprising, as there were a great many stars up in the deep blue over his head. However, they were of a different kind from the sort which were exploding in coloured lights before Bungo's eyes, so he shut them and just let himself drift. The water was also a great deal colder than he usually swam in at Queen's Mere, but he was young and healthy, with good thick fur, so that didn't worry him too much.

'Well, well, well,' said Bungo to himself,

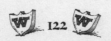

opening his eyes at last. 'I've escaped, that's what I've done. Fancy that.'

But even as he spoke he heard another sound. A soft sort of gulping sound. A kind of *splash, splash, splash, gulp* sound, which made him roll over on his stomach. Like nearly all the Wombles, he could see in the dark and he soon made out where the noise was coming from. Ahead of him was the dark shape he'd seen before. Quite a large round shape it was too, and behind it were a whole lot of smaller shapes. They were moving rapidly through the water, sending out a series of ripples, and Bungo was so interested – or curious – that he quite forgot to be afraid and began to paddle towards the Thing to get a closer look.

The Thing, whatever-it-was, didn't seem to notice Bungo until he was quite close, and then it suddenly ducked down into the loch with all its bumps and humps following it.

'Drat!' said Bungo crossly. Really the overalls he was wearing were nothing but an awful nuisance, they held him up so; and just when he had been about to discover something really interesting too. So he paddled back towards the shore and

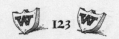

clambered out of the overalls and spread them on a bush, and then shook himself very thoroughly and plunged back into the loch.

Orinoco was still leaning up against the wall, trying to work out what was going on. Now that his stomach was quiet he could hear perfectly and, as all there was to hear was silence, he was getting more and more worried.

'Bungo, old chap, old friend,' he whispered, 'there's a monster in the loch. I know there is. It was in the newspaper, so it must be true. It probably eats Wombles and I shall never see you again. Oh dear, oh dear, oh my, oh my.'

There was a noise of pawsteps out in the passage, and Orinoco straightened up and just had the sense to drag off his own overalls and stuff them with straw and lay them on the floor beside his quaking, shivering self before the door was opened and a flaming torch was held aloft.

'All quiet,' said a gruff voice and the door was shut again and locked. Orinoco went on shaking and then got to his back paws and jumped up and down quite uselessly below the high window.

'Oh, I do wish I'd taken more exercise,' he

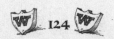

moaned. 'Oh, I do wish I wasn't *quite* so fat.' Remarks which Great Uncle Bulgaria and Tobermory would very much have appreciated. 'Oh, Bungo, do be careful, old chap. Please don't get eaten or anything.'

Bungo, completely unaware of his friend's fears, was paddling back across Loch Ness. He was really rather enjoying it, because he had a very inquisitive nature and he also had a very strong idea that he was, somehow, about to discover the Great Secret to which the MacWomble had referred in that mysterious way.

The shape had reappeared again with all its humps and bumps and was now swimming smoothly towards even deeper water.

'*Whoo-hoo*,' called Bungo, waving with one paw.

The shape stopped and turned round and looked at him and, even in the faint starlight, Bungo could see that it had a surprised expression on its face.

'Wait for me,' panted Bungo. He liked swimming, but it was quite a long haul from the shore and he was getting short of breath again, so he rolled over on his back and did a little gentle

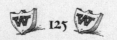

paddling with his paws. The shape seemed to hesitate and then stayed where it was while Bungo drew closer and closer, until he came right up alongside it and turned with a quick flip to look up at whatever-it-was.

'Hallo,' said Bungo. 'Who are you? I'm Bungo Womble from Wimbledon Common. In England, you know.'

A rather long, gentle face looked down at Bungo and then a very soft, sad voice said, 'How do you do. Pleased to make your acquaintance, I'm sure.'

Although it was a much more friendly voice, it had the same ups and downs in it as did the MacWomble's.

'Excuse me asking,' said Bungo, keeping himself afloat by just moving his paws, 'but are you – are you a Womble too?'

'Sort of,' replied the stranger, 'but a wee bit different from you Land-Wombles for all that. I'm a Water-Womble.'

'Well, I never,' said Bungo, turning a complete circle in his astonishment. 'Fancy that. I didn't know there were any. Well, I *say*!'

'Och,' said the Water-Womble, arching her neck,

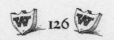

'there's no reason why you should. There's very few of us left, so they tell me. Just one or two clans around the world. You swim fine for a Land-Womble, so you do.'

'Oh, it's nothing, nothing at all,' said Bungo, trying to do another twist and misjudging it so that he came up choking and coughing. The Water-Womble put up a rather flat paw, or flipper, to politely hide a smile.

'So you're from England. How very interesting. Do you have many lochs down there?'

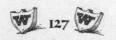

'Well, no, not really. We have lakes and ponds and things. Where I live we have a very fine stretch of water called Queen's Mere. Full of fish.'

'Is that right?'

The Water-Womble flapped both flippers on the surface and a whole line of bumps and humps appeared in the waters of the loch behind her, sending ripples further and further until they slapped against the banks.

'Right enough,' agreed Bungo, who felt that after his encounter with the MacWomble the Terrible he ought to stand up for the English Wombles. As bad at noticing things as Human Beings indeed! He'd show this Scottish lot! 'And ducks and a couple of otters too.'

'My, my,' said the Water-Womble, sighing in a somewhat melancholy manner. Bungo couldn't help glancing sideways at that long, long line of humps which must, surely, make his new friend the largest Womble in the whole world; but naturally he was far too polite to mention this, as it was only with really old friends, such as Orinoco and Tomsk, that one could make personal remarks about figure sizes.

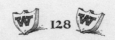

'We have a number of wild creatures up here too,' went on the Water-Womble. 'Deer, cats, goats, ponies and so forth, but we get along just fine. *They*'re not the ones who bother me.'

'Don't tell me you have trouble with the MacWomble,' exclaimed Bungo.

'Oh no,' the Water-Womble smiled faintly in the moonlight. 'He's my best friend.'

'He's very fierce though.'

'Not him. His talk's much sharper than his claws,' said the Water-Womble, reciting an old Womble saying which made Bungo feel suddenly homesick all over again. However, before he could ask any more questions there was a sudden stab of bright light over on one shore and the Water-Womble said quickly, 'Hold your breath, we're going down. Don't be scared now.'

Bungo just had time to do so as he was told before he found himself seized by the fur on the back of his neck and dragged under the water. Down was certainly the word, for he felt himself being propelled as though by a rocket as they raced through the black depths at a quite amazing speed. He shut his eyes and his mouth as tight as

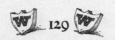

he could, and was just starting to feel panicky about drowning, when they changed course and a push from one powerful flipper sent him bobbing up to the surface.

'I do hope I haven't upset you,' said the Water-Womble, who seemed not at all out of breath from this fantastic burst of speed while Bungo, who hadn't swum at all but had been merely dragged along, was spluttering feebly. 'But it was them again.'

'Them?' Bungo managed to splutter.

'Human Beings – they just will not let me alone. Day and night they try and track me down with their wee boats and their fishing lines and nets and their spotter aircraft. They've even had a submarine going up and down the loch. They've no manners. No manners at all.'

'Why do they do it?' asked Bungo.

The searchlight was flickering over the loch about two miles away now and the Water-Womble gazed at it, sighing heavily in her mournful way.

'I've no idea. Last summer the whole road was lined with cars with people sitting in them

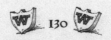

with their cameras. There were two film com-
panies here as well and goodness knows what
else. There's no peace these days. No peace at
all.'

'That's just what Great Uncle Bulgaria's always
saying,' agreed Bungo. 'We've got much the same
sort of problem at home, I can tell you. That's why
me and Orinoco – he's my friend – came up to
Scotland, to look for somewhere quieter.'

'I'd no advise you to try and settle here,' said
the Water-Womble. 'It's not at all a quiet place for
a burrow these days. Mind, it used to be; aye, it
was a grand place once and we could swim about
as much as we liked, with no one to bother us.
Now the only time we can really enjoy ourselves is
when it's raining hard or there's a nice thick loch
mist. Then we do manage to have a bit of fun. We
can even swim up to the shore and have a picnic.
The wee ones like that.'

'Are there – are there more of you?'

To Bungo's astonishment the Water-Womble
actually laughed so much at this question that it
was some minutes before he got his answer.

'Och, yes. Of course, there are. You didna think

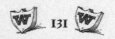

all of this was me, did you? Ross, Cromarty, come here now and meet your cousin from England.'

The last two of the humps and bumps ducked down into the water, vanished and then reappeared right in front of the paddling Bungo. They were slightly smaller than he was and had longer faces and sleeker, darker fur and webbed paws.

'Hallo,' they said together.

'How do you do.'

They shook paws politely and then one of the Water-Wombles gave the other a shove, which was returned with interest, and then both of them were rolling over and over and sending up showers of silvery spray.

'Now then, that'll be enough of that,' said the large Water-Womble, giving them both a gentle slap round the head. 'Och, well, Wombles will be Wombles and they've been hard at work all evening helping me to clear up the loch. Human Beings just dump anything in the water, you know. It's a sore problem and I couldn't manage to keep the place clean and tidy if it wasn't for the MacWomble. Ross, Cromarty, back into line, if you please. We've got the far shore to do yet.'

'I say,' said Bungo, as Ross and Cromarty, still pushing and shoving each other, went skimming back to take their places with the others. 'I say, there is just one small thing. You see – er – the MacWomble thinks Orinoco and me have come here to make trouble, but we honestly haven't, only he won't listen. He won't let us go home either and he's ordered us to stay here, but we can't. We must go back to Wimbledon Common and report. You couldn't help us, could you?'

There was silence while the Water-Womble gazed mournfully over the loch and Bungo waited with increasing breathlessness. In spite of all his training in Queen's Mere he was finding keeping himself afloat more and more tiring.

'I'm afraid not,' the Water-Womble said at last. 'It's a question of loyalty, you'll understand. The MacWomble is my friend. I couldn't go against his wishes. Mind, I could have a word on your behalf.'

'I'd be ever so grateful if you would,' said Bungo rather faintly.

'Poor wee thing, you're tired. Come along, you can have a ride on my back and I'll swim you to

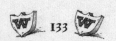

the shore. That light's gone off now, so we may be going to have a bit of peace. Up with you.'

It was like riding on a silent speedboat as they skimmed through the dark waters, and they were at the bank almost before Bungo had got his breath back.

'And how will you climb up there?' asked the Water-Womble, staring at the dark hole high in the bank.

'I can manage,' said Bungo, sliding down thankfully on to the wet but firm ground. 'We Wimbledon Wombles have to learn climbing properly, just like you do swimming and diving. Thank you very much for all your help.'

'It's been my pleasure. Goodnight to you. And as I said, I'll have a wee word with the MacWomble, but no promises, mind.'

'Aye. I mean yes.'

The Water-Womble began to slide deeper into the water and Bungo said in a hoarse whisper, 'I'm awfully sorry, but I don't know your name.'

'Ness,' replied the Water-Womble, 'after the loch, you see. Only round here they usually call me Nessie. Goodnight to you.'

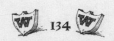

And the Loch Ness Womble submerged in the dark waters with scarcely a ripple, while Bungo stood waving on the shore.

CHAPTER 10

Wellington's Discovery

At round about the same time that all this was going on Wellington and Tomsk were also having their fair share of trouble. At 11.25 hours they had been deposited by Tobermory at Constitution Hill to one side of Buckingham Palace. It was, of course, a moonless night, just as it was in Scotland and, as the street lighting was not very bright in this part of London, Tobermory began to have faint hopes that Tomsk might just pass for a Grenadier Guardsman after all.

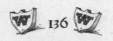

'Just remember,' he said, 'keep your mouth shut and let Wellington do all the talking. All you do is march up and down the way I taught you. Got that?'

Tomsk stared woodenly ahead and Tobermory said impatiently, 'You great gormless Womble. Do you understand?'

Tomsk remained silent.

'You told him not to speak,' said Wellington, who was unloading all his equipment out of the back of WOM I and setting it up, 'so he isn't. Right, Tomsk, old chap? You can nod, you know.'

Tomsk nodded violently and the black fur hat slid even further over his eyes, so that all he could see was his own boots and the wheels of the car.

'Well, I *suppose* it'll be all right,' said Tobermory doubtfully. 'I'll be back at seven thirty sharp. You haven't got long in which to work, young Wellington, so make the best of it and good luck. Remember, in an emergency you can use the Underground.'

Tobermory climbed back into the Silver Womble and, with a further wave of his paw, pulled away towards the great statue of Queen

Victoria which stands at the end of the Mall in front of the Palace. Both young Wombles felt very lost as they saw the car's lights vanish, and then Wellington remembered that he was in charge of this part of OWW and pulled himself together.

'Right-ho, Tomsk, old Womble,' he said, 'I'll set my stuff up right by the wall. No, don't help me. Soldiers don't help people with their tool bags, at least not while they're carrying a rifle.'

Tomsk looked hurt, but said nothing and Wellington who found this long silence unnerving, Wombles being such great talkers, went on hurriedly, 'You can talk to *me*, you know. Only not strangers.'

'What are you doing, Wellington?'

'Digging.'

'Why? I can't see much of you, you know, only your back paws and that lantern. Why do you need a lantern anyway? You can see in the dark, can't you?'

'It's to *show* that I'm digging,' said Wellington, who was starting to think that perhaps, after all, Tomsk's silence had been better than all these questions.

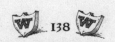

'But I thought we were supposed to be doing all this secretly,' said Tomsk, becoming more and more puzzled.

'Well, we are and we aren't.'

Wellington put down the small shovel and paused to wipe his round spectacles, which had become misted up with his efforts. He had put up the small fence so that he could hide between it and the Palace garden wall, and had placed the red WBC lantern beside it. Tomsk was standing at ease in front of this and in the lantern's soft glow he gave Wellington quite a start. It was astonishing how 'real' dear old Tomsk looked!

'Go on,' said Tomsk.

'What we are *really* doing is secret,' said Wellington, 'but what we're pretending to do isn't. Now do you understand?'

There was a longish pause.

'No,' said Tomsk regretfully.

'Never mind. I'm going to start digging again. Just keep your eyes open.'

'It doesn't matter how open they are, all I can see is the edge of my hat. It must be jolly difficult to fight in these clothes, you know. You can hardly move at all and you wouldn't know the enemy soldier was there until he was about a foot away from you. Still I suppose if he was wearing the same kind of uniform, it would make things just as difficult for him. Their battles must look very odd, don't you think?'

'Um,' said Wellington who was working away in a frenzy, sending up showers of earth behind him. Like all the Wombles he was extremely good at digging for they are burrowing creatures; but whoever had built this wall had made a very good job of it. Lower and lower and lower he went and the sound of an occasional car swishing past and of Tomsk's droning voice grew fainter and fainter, until practically all he could hear was his own fast breathing.

'Down and down and down we go,' Wellington muttered to himself. '*Whoops*, hallo, this is it . . .'

He paused as his busy little paws touched not stone but soft, familiar earth and at the same moment he thought he heard a voice, a strange voice, up above his head. For a second Wellington was tempted to stay safely where he was in this nice comforting burrow he had built, but then he remembered that he was SD 3 and that Great Uncle Bulgaria was relying on him, so he took a deep breath and scrabbled his way up the tunnel at top speed just in time to catch the words '. . . is going on here, eh?'

Wellington's head appeared over the top of the small fence and he saw, standing in front of Tomsk, the figure of a large London policeman. Wellington's fur prickled and his heart thundered as he had a sudden picture of Tomsk and himself being marched away to the Tower of London.

'Evening, officer,' said Wellington in a high voice.

'And who might you be?'

'Ministry of Works,' said Wellington, realising that he couldn't remember the words which Tobermory had drummed into him earlier that day.

'Emergency repairs to the wall. Care to have a look?' he added with enormous daring.

The policeman glanced at Tomsk who was motionless as a rock and then trod over heavily to the small fence and peered down.

'My word,' he said, 'that's some hole, that is.'

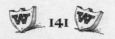

'Not bad, is it?' agreed Wellington proudly. 'I mean, it's quite a big burrow.'

'*Burrow?*'

'Rats,' said Wellington desperately. 'Rats burrow terrible holes, you know.'

'Yes.' The policeman seemed unconvinced. He stared at the tunnel and then at Wellington who was carefully keeping in Tomsk's large shadow, and then at the lamp.

'Funny,' said the policeman, 'it's got WBC on it.'

For one sickening moment Wellington felt his mind go completely blank and then to his astonishment he heard his own voice say, 'Windsor and Balmoral Castles. I didn't have time to get a Buckingham Palace lantern. Emergency job, like I said.'

'Ah,' said the policeman, as though this did in fact explain everything. 'Take long to deal with, will it?'

'Oh no, just another few hours,' said Wellington, feeling almost faint with relief. 'But I'd better get back to it or I'll have Great Uncle Bulgaria after me.'

'Great Uncle . . . ?'

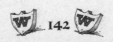

'The Chief. That's what we call him.'

'There's no respect these days, young feller-me-lad,' said the policeman severely. 'Just you watch your tongue.' And he walked off slowly up Constitution Hill muttering to himself under his breath, 'Calling your boss "Great Uncle Bulgaria" indeed. I don't know what the world's coming to . . .'

'I say, that *was* quick,' said Tomsk in a low whisper. 'Saying it was rats. I'd never have thought of that, Wellington.'

'Um.'

Wellington waited for a short while to allow his fur to lie down and then wiped his spectacles with trembling paws.

'I'm through,' he said softly, 'and I'm going into the garden in a minute. Now listen carefully, Tomsk. If another policeman comes along, or anyone else for that matter, and begins trying to talk to you, march up and down and STAMP. Stamp good and loud and with any luck I'll hear you and come back. All right?'

'Yes, Wellington.'

'Here goes then,' said Wellington and vanished

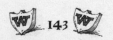

down the tunnel. There were a few faint, scuffling noises from him and then silence, and Tomsk felt a shiver of apprehension. He was so used to other Wombles telling him what to do – unless he was playing golf – that he was not at all sure he was going to be able to manage on his own.

The time seemed to drag past and, as there was less and less traffic, he hadn't even got the sound of many passing cars to count. He did notice though that there were no heavy lorries on this road, which was one good thing to report to Great Uncle Bulgaria. There was, however, quite a bit of wildlife in the park opposite him. He couldn't see it, of course, because of his hat; but he could sense it all right and it made him feel almost at home. All the same it wasn't half as nice as his own Wimbledon Common and Tomsk sighed sadly . . .

Slowly the hours passed and he must have dozed off while standing at ease, for the next thing he knew was that yet another Human Being had stopped in front of him and was saying briskly, 'Asleep on duty, my good man?'

Tomsk snapped to attention and began to count under his breath, 'One, two, three, FOUR. One,

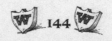

two, three, FOUR', as he brought his rifle smartly up against his shoulder and then over it.

'One, two.'

Tomsk turned on his heel, banged his paws together with all his might and then counted again, 'One, two, three, FOUR.'

Bang, bang. Tomsk's boots thumped on the ground as he began to march up and down before the small fence. He was making an enormous amount of noise – surely Wellington must hear him?

'Very smart,' agreed the man, keeping step with Tomsk. 'All right, guardsman, attention. Right turn. Stand at ease. Stand easy.'

Oh my, oh my, oh my! thought Tomsk, feeling grateful for the first time that so much of his face was hidden. One thing he had found simple to learn was the drill Tobermory had taught him. He seemed to be doing it right, too, and it was a shame that there were no Wombles there to watch him.

'I'm on plain clothes duty,' said the man and he flipped open an important-looking card so that Tomsk by squinting downwards could just see it.

'Had a report about you being here earlier on. I'd just like your name and serial number.'

Tomsk, who had not the slightest idea what this meant, stared straight ahead. Oh, why didn't Wellington come? Or Tobermory, as it was growing light?

'Come along, come along,' the man said impatiently. 'Name?'

'Tomsk,' said Tomsk hoarsely.

'Thomas?' said the man. 'First name?'

'That is my first name. Tomsk Womble.'

'*Really*? Oh! Number?'

'SD 6,' said Tomsk desperately.

'Never heard of a number like *that* before.'

'It stands for Special Duties,' said Tomsk even more hoarsely. 'SD 6, OWW.'

'Very interesting. I thought these buttons of yours weren't quite right,' the man said and wrote busily in a notebook. Tomsk took the chance to come to attention again, to shoulder his rifle with a good loud *slap*, *slap*, and then to resume his marching. The man put away his notebook and fell into step with him, saying, 'I didn't realise you were one of the Special Duties lot. Sorry.

Interesting jobs you chaps get. OWW, eh? Well, well. I wouldn't mind trying to get into your line of work myself. Difficult, is it?'

'Very,' said Tomsk with real feeling.

STAMP, STAMP, STAMP.

'Ah well. Good night, chum,' and the man went off towards the Mall just as Wellington's face appeared over the top of the fence.

'Trouble?' he whispered. 'What did he want?'

'*I* don't know,' said Tomsk. 'I didn't understand a word he said and I don't believe he understood a word *I* said either. And anyway what's the matter with my buttons? They've got very nice anchors on them.'

'Oh, don't worry about that now,' said Wellington, who was tired out and suffering from a deep disappointment. 'It's nearly half past seven and Tobermory'll be here soon and I've got to fill up this beastly, rotten tunnel.'

'What's the matter with you?'

'Nothing,' said Wellington untruthfully and returned to work. He had just finished neatly stamping down the earth and was folding up the fence when WOM 1 drew up with a quiet swish.

Tomsk couldn't resist presenting arms with a flourish and Tobermory smiled faintly, although like Wellington he looked extremely tired.

'Don't tell me about it now,' he said as they moved away through the already thickening traffic and Tomsk could at last remove his helmet and give his head a really good scratch. 'You'll have to report it all to Great Uncle Bulgaria anyway.'

Great Uncle Bulgaria was waiting for them in the Operations Room, and his face lit up as he saw them.

'Well?' he asked eagerly.

'It's no good,' said Wellington wearily. 'It's a lovely garden all right and there's a nice big lake for swimming in, but there wouldn't be anything for us to *do*. You've never seen such a tidy place. Not a bus ticket or a milk carton or a glove in sight. No food either.'

There was a heavy silence which was broken by Great Uncle Bulgaria saying hopefully, 'Perhaps they'd just had a clean-up. After all, think of the Garden Parties . . .'

Wellington shook his head and tried to fight down an enormous yawn. The splendid adventure

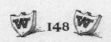

was over and it had been a dismal failure — not that it was his fault exactly, but it was disappointing.

'Just before I left this morning,' he said, 'some corgi dogs came into the garden with a small boy. Nice little chap he was, friendly, so I had a word with him. You don't mind, do you?'

'No,' said Great Uncle Bulgaria and then sat up with a start and added anxiously, 'a small . . . ? I hope you bowed, young Womble?'

'Oh yes. So did he. Very good manners he had for a Human Being. He told me that the gardens were *always* tidy. It seems that there are special people who do the cleaning and clearing up which is nice for him, of course, because he never loses his toys. Or at least not for loooooooooong . . .'

Wellington put up his paw to try and hide a really tremendous yawn. Tomsk was already fast asleep sitting bolt upright in his chair.

'Oh well, that's that then,' said Great Uncle Bulgaria. 'It can't be helped. You were right, Tobermory, it was an impractical idea, although not perhaps for the reasons you had thought of. You've done a fine night's work, the pair of you.

Don't think of this as the failure of a mission but rather . . .'

'Ah-HEM,' said Tobermory.

'But rather as a very good attempt,' went on Great Uncle Bulgaria. 'Now off to bed, the pair of you. Or do you want breakfast first?'

'No, thank you,' said Wellington, pulling the still slumbering Tomsk to his feet. 'We didn't have time to eat that snack during the night so we had it in the car coming back. Oh – I nearly forgot.'

And Wellington let go of Tomsk, who would have toppled over if Tobermory hadn't caught him and lowered him on to his chair again.

'That reminds me. Those Human Beings aren't all that good at clearing up. I did find one thing.' Wellington burrowed into the bottom of the picnic box and closed his small dirty paw round something, which he then laid carefully before Great Uncle Bulgaria.

It was a small object, but it glittered and glowed and flashed with coloured lights as it lay on the desk.

'*Tsk, tsk, tsk!*' said Great Uncle Bulgaria in such a funny way that Tobermory turned round from the

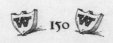

big map where he had been neatly removing two red-topped drawing pins from the gardens of Buckingham Palace.

'It *is* pretty, isn't it?' said Wellington. 'I've never seen anything so pretty before in my whole life.'

'You wouldn't have,' said Great Uncle Bulgaria slowly, 'because, you daft young Womble, this is one of Her diamond brooches, I shouldn't be surprised.'

'Oh,' said Wellington faintly.

'Oh, indeed,' agreed Great Uncle Bulgaria, gazing thoughtfully at the glittering diamonds. 'The question is, what do we do about it?'

CHAPTER II

Troubles

'We now have three problems instead of one,' said Great Uncle Bulgaria. 'Troubles always do seem to come in threes, I don't know why. Well, Tobermory old friend, what's to be done?'

They had all of them slept through most of the day and were now feeling a little less low in spirit, and more able to deal with the difficulties which lay ahead. The life of the burrow was going fairly

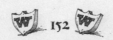

smoothly, although in a rather makeshift way. Miss Adelaide had put Forms Two and Three on duty in the Workshop, to sort out all the objects which had been collected during the night by the ordinary working Wombles shift; and Tobermory had placed Lookout Wombles in two passages where there had been a further downwards movement during the last eight hours. Tomsk was still asleep with his back paws higher than his head, but Wellington had returned to the Operations Room and was all ready to take notes.

'First things first, I suppose,' said Tobermory. 'And to my way of thinking that means Bungo and Orinoco. I've got a young Womble in hiding near the telephone box – just in case a call should come through, but somehow I don't think we're going to hear anything . . .'

'It'll take a lot to defeat young Bungo,' said Great Uncle Bulgaria firmly. 'Silly sort of name, Bungo, but he's quite a bright Womble in his way. Right then, somebody must follow in their pawsteps to find out exactly what they are up to!'

Wellington glanced up nervously. Looking back on it, last night had not been quite so terrifying

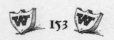

really, but all the same he didn't feel up to another adventure just yet.

'Who shall it be?' said Great Uncle Bulgaria, frowning over the top of his spectacles.

'Me,' said Tobermory simply. 'We've got nobody else trained and it's too soon to send Wellington and Tomsk out again. I could take the Silver Womble and drive up. If we can spare the money for more nettle and acorn juice?'

'We *are* getting low,' Great Uncle Bulgaria agreed, scratching his ear and, just for a moment, his old eyes rested on the sweet tin which now held the diamond brooch and had 'HM(?)' painted on the lid. There, in a way, lay a fortune which could be the solution to many of their problems. But no, he, Bulgaria Coburg Womble, must not have such dark thoughts, so he went on, 'But Wombles are more important than money and, thank goodness, Human Beings being the careless creatures that they are, we are sure to go on finding coins left behind on the Common. Very well, Tobermory, you shall travel up to Loch Ness – at least we know they got *that* far. But I don't think it would be wise for you to go alone. You must take another Womble with you. Who would you like as a companion?'

Tobermory thought deeply, while a lorry thundered towards Tibbet's Corner and a worried young Womble in one of the suspect passages watched nervously as the floor creaked downwards.

'Miss Adelaide,' said Tobermory at last and then, seeing Great Uncle Bulgaria's enquiring look, he went on, 'She may not be as young as she was, but she's reliable.'

'Agreed. Very well, I'll have a word with her after supper if there has been no call by then. You'll drive up by night?'

Tobermory nodded and Wellington let out a very faint sigh of relief, as he was secretly very glad that it wasn't going to be him.

'Next,' said Great Uncle Bulgaria, tapping the sweet tin, 'this. I had better deal with it, I think.'

'It might be dangerous,' protested Tobermory. 'They might think that it had been stolen. *We* know that Wombles never steal, but they don't.'

'I'll be all right,' said Great Uncle Bulgaria serenely, 'and it must be returned. The sooner the

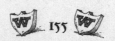

better. I shall see to it first thing in the morning.'

'How will you get there?' Wellington couldn't help asking.

Great Uncle Bulgaria thought of the stiffness of his old back paws and how very nice it would be to travel by taxi. But they couldn't afford it and that was that.

'Underground to St James's Park,' he said shortly. 'Finally, regarding the Operation Wandering Womble, Fresh Fields and Pastures New,' and his bright old eyes rested thoughtfully on Wellington, who felt distinctly apprehensive. Great Uncle Bulgaria got up slowly and went over to him, resting one paw on Wellington's now quivering shoulder.

'You,' he said, 'have been a member of OWW from almost its beginnings. You're an intelligent young Womble and since last night I think you've gained some confidence. I want you to study this map of the London area *only*' – and he shot a look at Tobermory who was smiling slightly – 'as time is short and we cannot, alas, look further afield. See if you can think of a solution, however temporary, to our problem. We need a new home, young Womble, and quickly.'

'Very quickly,' agreed Tobermory, who had felt the recent subsidence in his bones.

'Sir!' said Wellington, getting to his feet and dropping his notebook on the floor. He had felt rather low about the failure of last night's mission, but now knowing that, in spite of having made the awful mistake of bringing back the brooch, Great Uncle Bulgaria still trusted him, he felt better again.

'That's all right, young Womble,' said Great Uncle Bulgaria, 'we all make mistakes. I made one too. Never be ashamed to admit it. Very well then, that's the end of the meeting. Dismiss.'

As, of course, there was no telephone message from Bungo and Orinoco, the next few hours were very busy. Miss Adelaide took the news that she was to travel up to Scotland in search of the missing pair in her usual calm manner, and went off to have a word with the oldest small Womble in the Womblegarten. A word which left him feeling very grown-up and responsible and also rather scared, as he had been told extremely firmly that, if as much as one bus ticket was left lying about in the Workshop, Miss Adelaide would want to know the reason why!

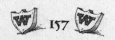

Great Uncle Bulgaria spent his time talking to Madame Cholet and explaining that for a few hours at least she would be in sole charge of the Wimbledon Wombles.

'I see,' said Madame Cholet. 'Don't give it another thought. They know that I am the one who gets their meals and, Wombles being Wombles and very fond of their stomachs, they'll do exactly as I say, do not doubt it, Bulgaria.'

'I don't,' said Great Uncle Bulgaria and chuckled for the first time in a very long while. He felt very proud of his Wombles as he saw how well they were rallying round, and, if he was at all worried about what was going to happen to himself in the morning, he certainly did not show it. But he did write a little note and leave it in his desk – just in case he should not return.

At midnight Miss Adelaide and Tobermory set off in the Silver Womble. All the working Wombles, who were out on the Common clearing up the litter which had been left behind by the Human Beings earlier in the day, waved to them as they purred past and Miss Adelaide bowed graciously.

The parting between the three oldest Wombles had been brief and to the point. Great Uncle Bulgaria had shaken the paws of Miss Adelaide and Tobermory and wished them 'good luck' and Tobermory had replied, 'And you be careful.'

And Miss Adelaide had said, 'See you within the month, Bulgaria.'

And that had been that.

Once the sun had risen Great Uncle Bulgaria, who had not slept particularly well, had a quick cup of nettle tea with Madame Cholet. Having

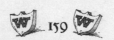

politely refused her offer of a packet of sandwiches for the journey, he set off for the
Underground station at Wimbledon. When he
reached the edge of the Common he paused and
looked over his shoulder for a moment and then
braced his old shoulders. Even if he was not
believed, but accused of stealing Very Important
Jewels, his Wombles would be able to manage
without him. No Womble, after all, was indispen-
sable and there were plenty of young ones who
would be able to plan ahead. All the same it was
rather unsettling to realise that, out of all the
older ones, only Madame Cholet was left behind.

'Don't go getting fanciful,' Great Uncle Bulgaria
said sternly to himself. He turned up the collar of
the overcoat which he had taken from the stores
and, leaning rather heavily on his stick, entered
Wimbledon Station.

While all this was happening, deep down in the
Operations Room Wellington was already on duty
and busy, not only studying the map but also looking through several very interesting old books and
papers which, as librarian before he became SD 3,
he had read once before.

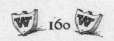

'Very interesting,' Wellington murmured to himself. 'I wonder . . .'

'Hallo,' said Tomsk, putting his head round the door and beaming. 'Talking to yourself, are you? You know what that's supposed to be a sign of, don't you?' and he tapped one large paw against the side of his head.

'Shut up and come in,' said Wellington. 'I say, Tomsk, old Womble, I've had an idea. Remember last night?'

'I shan't ever forget it,' said Tomsk, 'not ever. All those questions. You don't think I was wrong do you to tell that Human Being I was SD 6 from OWW?'

'No, of course not. He didn't know what you meant – he was just pretending to, I bet. My guess would be that he didn't want to let you know that he didn't. If you follow me?'

'No, I don't,' said Tomsk after a long, thoughtful pause.

'Exactly,' beamed Wellington, taking off his spectacles. 'Well, never mind that now. You told me that when you were on sentry duty . . .'

'Sentry what?'

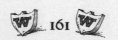

'Marching up and down.'

'Oh yes. One, two, three, FOUR.'

'Yes, that bit. Well, that you felt that there were a lot of wild animals about.'

'Oh, I did. I did,' said Tomsk, nodding wisely. 'Rabbits and rats and field mice, and there were some owls too. Funny, isn't it, in the middle of London?'

'Very funny. Now look at this map here. That's where you were facing. You had your back to Buckingham Palace Gardens and you were looking at Green . . .'

'I wasn't looking at anything really,' Tomsk interrupted earnestly, 'because I couldn't *see*.'

'Well, if you could have seen you would have been looking at Green Park. There. On the map, that green bit. And beyond that is Hyde Park and further north still is Regent's Park. Right?'

'Yes,' said Tomsk, nodding slowly. 'I say, Wellington, isn't there a lot of green bits in London?'

'Yes, there is. I mean are. They're where Human Beings go to have picnics and walks and school outings.'

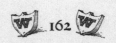

'Just like Wimbledon Common,' agreed Tomsk.

'Well, almost. I think this could be the answer to our problem.'

'What problem?'

Wellington looked at his large friend and was about to answer rather crossly, when he remembered how well Tomsk had managed to deal with that very inquisitive Human Being the night before, so he kept his temper and only said, 'The problem of where we're going to live.'

'Oh, *that*,' said Tomsk happily. 'Bungo and Orinoco are finding that out. Although,' and he sighed so heavily that the map almost flew off the wall, 'although I wish we didn't have to move at all. I *like* it here.'

Even as he spoke there was a tremendous rumbling noise on the Common and all the walls shook and then, very slowly, the map really did come away from the drawing pins and shook itself down on the ground; and at the same time there was a horrible creaking, cracking sound above their heads, and a piece of plaster crashed down on the desk and splintered into dust all over Great Uncle Bulgaria's papers. There was a moment's terrible silence, as though every living creature was holding its breath, and then a dreadful, terrifying *CRASH* which was followed by a horrifying scream.

Wellington and Tomsk, as though turned into statues, stood staring at each other for a moment, and then rushed for the door of the Operations Room and tugged at the handle.

'It won't move,' grunted Wellington, pulling with all his might.

'Yes, it jolly well will,' snorted Tomsk, and pushed his friend out of the way and caught hold of the handle himself and tugged. The next moment he was lying on his back with the handle still in his paws while the door remained tightly closed.

'Look, look,' cried Wellington, pointing up at the ceiling which had started to bulge downwards in a very nasty way.

'The ladders,' panted Tomsk, 'put the ladders there and some books on top – that will hold it.'

Wellington did as he was told, picking up the largest and heaviest volumes he could lay his paws on, as there came another ominous *CREAK*.

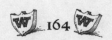

It was dreadful, like the end of the world with everything collapsing round them, and suddenly he had a horrible picture of the whole burrow falling down and himself and Tomsk being buried.

'The door,' panted Tomsk, 'come on, Wellington, quick, quick, we must get the door open.' And Tomsk pushed his great shoulders against it with all his strength, while outside the cries and shouts grew louder and louder as the earth above the burrow of the Wimbledon Wombles slowly started to cave in on itself.

CHAPTER 12

Bungo Is Happy Again

'I don't know what you're so cheerful about,' grumbled Orinoco. Although the Scottish Wombles had a very good cook he was suffering from pangs of homesickness which even four square meals a day could not get rid of.

It was true that the Clan Womble treated their English cousins with great politeness; even going so far as to offer to teach them to play the bag-

pipes – an honour that Bungo and Orinoco had declined as gracefully as they could.

'Imagine Great Uncle Bulgaria's face if we started making that row during supper!' said Bungo.

'It'd be worth it just to see his face again,' replied Orinoco with awful melancholy.

However, it was also true that in spite of all this the Wimbledon Wombles were under guard; and since the night that Bungo had slipped into the loch and had the interesting conversation with Nessie, he had made no further attempts to escape.

'Impossible,' he said briefly. 'I had a look round, naturally, but the MacWomble's got patrols everywhere. Nearly fell right on top of one of them, I did. Not that they were looking for you and me; it's just that they have to be careful with all these strange Human Beings about. Funny they should be so curious about poor Nessie when they never take any notice of us at all . . .'

Bungo, in fact, and much to Orinoco's concern, seemed to have settled down quite happily and would keep smiling to himself in a most irritating manner, which was what roused Orinoco to add peevishly, 'You've changed sides, that's what it is.

You've deserted the Wimbledon Wombles for the Clan.'

'It isn't anything to do with sides,' Bungo explained patiently. 'We're all Wombles under our fur, even Nessie and Ross and Cromarty and all the rest of them. It's just that the MacWomble feels he's got to be extra careful all the time. He told me that his fur still prickles now and again when he thinks what might have happened if we had been stopped and questioned by some Human Beings when we were riding through Scotland.'

'The MacWomble seems to tell you a lot of things,' said Orinoco, now sounding thoroughly put out.

'Well, he doesn't frighten me so much since Nessie said his talk was sharper than his claws. He's rather like Tobermory really. You know how *he* snaps at one sometimes, but he doesn't mean it.'

'I wish he was snapping at me this very minute.'

'*If wishes were horses then Wombles would ride,*' quoted Bungo.

'Oh, shut up,' growled Orinoco and went off to have a word with the cook whose kitchen,

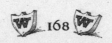

although larger (as it had once been a cave), was not half as cosy and cheerful as Madame Cholet's. Bungo watched him leave and scratched his ear thoughtfully.

He was mainly cheerful because, after meeting Nessie, he had done one or two rather odd things while carefully avoiding the Clan patrols. He thought that what he had done might well lead to himself and Orinoco being rescued, but he wasn't absolutely sure. And, being Bungo, part of him wanted to take a lot of the credit for the surprise which could happen, and part of him didn't want his old friend Orinoco getting too excited and then being disappointed.

'Oh, well,' said Bungo, 'ho-hum.'

Under guard or not, both the Wimbledon Wombles were expected to work like everyone else, and they were taken out in separate working parties to clear up all the litter with which the road beside the loch was covered regularly.

'Astonishing what they leave behind, isn't it?' said Bungo to Culvain, a young Womble of about his own age with whom he had struck up quite a friendship.

'Aye,' replied Culvain, who like Tomsk was usually a Womble of few words.

'This is a funny-looking coin,' said Bungo, who was anxious to have a bit of a breather. In spite of all their training on Wimbledon Common, he and Orinoco were not nearly as fit and tough as the members of the Clan, who could scamper up and down the mountains all night without getting tired.

'American,' said Culvain. 'We've a grand number of American visitors during the summer. And they're aye grand folk for leaving their belongings about. Good stuff it is too.'

This was practically a speech for him and it gave Bungo a chance to have a few moments' more rest.

'That's just what Cousin Yellowstone Womble said,' exclaimed Bungo. 'He came over from the States to visit us once, you know.'

'Aye, you told me.'

The rest period was obviously over, for Culvain was already moving away, slipping as easily through the bushes as Nessie and her Water-Wombles slid through the loch. Bungo sighed and hitched his basketful of handkerchiefs, gloves, one

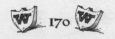

camera, two films, three biros, one torch, two Thermos flasks, one screwdriver (which made him think of Tobermory) and three pairs of spectacles (which made him think of Great Uncle Bulgaria) more firmly over his arm, and then went sliding and slipping down the slope after his Scottish cousin.

He was still sliding somewhat ungracefully on his seat, when Culvain appeared out of nowhere, or so it seemed, and dragged him roughly into the bushes.

'Look here, um, um, um,' muttered Bungo as a paw was clamped over his mouth.

'Shut up and listen.'

Bungo glared, but did as he was told and sure enough, travelling slowly down the road which was only a few yards below them, came a large grey car. It had a very quiet engine and, because of its colour, was almost hidden by the early morning mists which were wreathing down the valley. Bungo might have slid right into it, but Culvain's Highland ears had heard it easily.

'Um, um, um,' rumbled Bungo.

'Will you be quiet!'

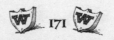

'UM!' replied Bungo and suddenly, to Culvain's dismay, Bungo wrenched himself free and went off bumping and jumping and yelling at the top of his voice until he reached the road. The car had moved on but Bungo went after it, twirling his basket over his head as he ran.

'Mad,' whispered Culvain, setting off after Bungo. 'The wee Womble's gone off his head!'

'Yoo-hoo,' shouted Bungo, sending various wild animals streaking for cover and startling even Nessie out on the loch, so that she dived for deep water instantly. 'Yooooooo-hooooooo!'

Up and down the mountainsides Wombles everywhere heard the din and stopped working. It shattered the peace of Carn na Saobhaidhe and Glen Urquhart, it sent a shiver of fright through the fur of a small Womble at Loch Duntelchaig and it even reached the ears of an old grey Womble chief out at Carn Eige.

'It's a war cry sure enough,' he muttered to himself. 'The Clans must be gathering,' and he moved off extremely fast, for one of his age, to get his own North-west Highland Wombles together.

News travels fast in this part of Scotland as all

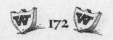

the Highland Wombles had scouts posted. This is because they often got lonely out on the mountains as there are not many of them and whenever possible they like to get together for a good gossip. So information was passed from loch to loch and mountain to mountain and valley to valley at quite an astonishing rate.

Bungo, completely unaware of what he had started, was still panting after the car and, although it was travelling at only ten miles an hour, he would never have caught it (as naturally even in his excitement he was still hanging on to his basket), if one of the occupants of the car had not said, 'Wait. I think we are being followed.'

'Very well,' replied the driver and stopped.

'What beautiful scenery,' said the passenger. 'Such grandeur. It is all *most* impressive.'

'Very fine, if you like that kind of thing,' said the driver. 'I prefer a flatter kind of place myself.'

'We must not let our preferences blind us to the beauty of our surroundings,' the passenger said severely.

'Oh, oh *quite*,' agreed the driver.

'Here he comes,' said the passenger as a small,

rather tubby figure appeared round a corner in the road.

'Yoo-hoo,' said Bungo, panting dreadfully as he reached the car. 'It's me, you know.'

'So I see,' said Miss Adelaide calmly, 'and about time too. We have been following your trail for the last thirty minutes at least.'

'And where have you been?' growled Tobermory. 'Put that basket down, young Womble, before you drop it. Out of training, that's your trouble.'

'Oh, I AM glad to see you,' said Bungo, sniffing and panting at the same time. 'I thought you'd *never* come!'

'Don't be silly, dear,' said Miss Adelaide, 'you should know better than to think that we would ever desert a Wimbledon Womble. And WHO is this?'

'It's my friend, Culvain,' said Bungo, who was leaning against WOM I and smiling from ear to ear. Oh, how wonderful, how marvellous it was to be ticked off by Tobermory and Miss Adelaide. Why, any moment now Tobermory would tell him not to be more foolish than he could help, and Miss Adelaide would ask to see if his paws were dirty.

'Good morning, Culvain,' said Miss Adelaide. 'You may get into the back of the car, but please wipe your paws before you do so. They appear to be extremely muddy.'

'Aye,' said Culvain, 'och aye. Yes, mistress.'

'Come along, come along,' said Tobermory, who was not going to show his enormous relief at finding Bungo in front of some Foreign Womble, 'haven't got all day, you know. The sun'll be up properly in a moment, I shouldn't wonder. Stop behaving like a couple of foolish young Wombles and hop in, do!'

Bungo and Culvain hopped.

The MacWomble, as befitted the occasion, received his English visitors in the Great Hall. He wasn't too sure how to deal with the situation, so he sat in his carved chair and tried to look as fierce as possible as Miss Adelaide and Tobermory were shown in, followed by Bungo and Orinoco who were, of course, unable to stop themselves from grinning from ear to ear.

'Welcome,' said the MacWomble.

'Good morning,' said Miss Adelaide.

'How do you do,' said Tobermory.

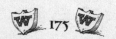

'Good day to you both. I suppose,' the MacWomble glared at the grinning Bungo, 'I suppose you realise what you've done? You've roused the Clans. There'll be Highland Wombles coming down the glen from all over Scotland.'

'Oh my! Oh dear!' said Bungo.

Orinoco said nothing at all, as nothing in the world would, at that moment, have made him stop smiling. He could only gaze and gaze at the straight back of Miss Adelaide and the screwdriver which, as usual, was tucked behind Tobermory's ear.

'Indeed?' said Miss Adelaide. 'How very fortunate. Then Tobermory and I shall be able to meet a large number of our Scottish cousins. I am sure it will be most enjoyable.'

'Och, well,' said the MacWomble, rather at a loss for words. 'I dare say, but . . .'

'I,' said Miss Adelaide, looking him up and down, chair and all, as if the MacWomble was a member of the Womblegarten, 'should be very glad of some breakfast. And I expect Tobermory feels the same, don't you?'

And she gave Tobermory a sharp dig in the ribs.

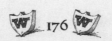

176

Tobermory, who had been looking round the hall and shaking his head and muttering to himself, nodded. Then he pulled his notebook and pencil out of his apron pocket, made a few quick notes and looked severely at the MacWomble.

'*Tsk, tsk, tsk*,' he said. 'I don't like the look of those rafters, or that doorway. Half underwater here, aren't you! Well,' not waiting for an answer, 'you'll get subsidence if you don't watch out. Bungo, take one end of this tape measure. Orinoco – my word, you've put on a bit of weight, have to see about that – you take the other.'

'Yes, Tobermory,' said Bungo, beaming more than ever.

'The Clans Are Gathering, I said,' roared the MacWomble, who was starting to feel very strongly that things were not going at all as he had planned.

'Good,' said Tobermory absent-mindedly. 'That's fifteen yards exactly, Bungo. Good, you're going to need all the paws you can get to help you.'

'Not until they've had breakfast,' said Miss Adelaide, looking at the MacWomble in a way which made his fur shiver a little.

'Och, very well,' said the MacWomble and clapped his paws. 'But later on I'll need to know just how you found these two.'

'Quite simple,' said Miss Adelaide. 'One of them left tracking marks all the way beside the loch. Not very *good* tracking marks, but quite sufficient as it has turned out.'

For once the MacWomble was completely bereft of words, but Orinoco, who was now scrambling round the Great Hall in a very professional manner, nudged his old friend and whispered, 'I say, Bungo, well done.'

'It was nothing,' Bungo replied modestly. 'I did it that night I met Nessie. I remembered what we'd been taught as scouts and . . .'

'Bungo,' shouted that splendidly gruff, familiar voice, 'hold the tape steady, you silly young Womble.'

'Yes, Tobermory,' said Bungo happily, and did as he was told without further ado.

CHAPTER 13

The Wandering Wombles

The moment he reached the edge of the Common, Great Uncle Bulgaria sensed that something was wrong. Up till that moment he had been like a Womble in a dream, murmuring to himself, 'How *very* gracious, how *truly* kind ...' in a way that had made the other occupants of the railway carriage move slowly to the far end of the compartment.

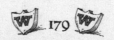

However, Great Uncle Bulgaria had been utterly unaware of this, for his old white head had been spinning with the affairs of the morning. It had all been so unexpected, so completely contrary to anything he could have anticipated. The courteous manner in which he had been received, the somewhat unnerving wait in the anteroom, during which he had pictured himself in the Tower of London, and then the sudden alarming summons. The walk down that long, long corridor, the very polite Human Being who had announced him in such ringing tones, 'Mr Bulgaria Coburg Womble . . .'

The door had shut behind him and that very gentle yet clear voice had spoken to him. Something, he couldn't quite recall now, about having 'heard of him and the Wimbledon Wombles from a certain young gentleman . . .'

Heard of *him*, Bulgaria Womble! And of his Wimbledon Wombles! It was almost too much! And yet there had been still more to come. He had bent low over an extended hand, had been asked to Sit Down and had actually Talked to Her. He had even told Her, he now remembered, how – as a very young Womble and wearing a cap with HMS *DREADNOUGHT* on it – he had waved a flag when Her great-great-grandmother had attended a parade of Her troops on Wimbledon Common. She had been most interested in that! And when he had presented the sweet tin with 'HM(?)' on it, She had not only smiled, She had laughed!

And furthermore . . .

Great Uncle Bulgaria's beautiful memories faded at this point. He paused on the edge of the Common and his white fur stood up on end. He stared at the changed landscape and then, forgetting everything else, he hobbled across the grass as fast as he could go. One of the back doors, mercifully still well hidden by bushes, was swinging on its hinges. He gave it a push and entered the burrow, his stick tapping on the now uneven surface, and almost immediately a very anxious, dusty Womble face appeared.

'Oh, Great Uncle Bulgaria! Oh dear, oh my, oh dear . . . !'

'Now then, keep calm, young Wellington,' said Great Uncle Bulgaria severely. 'Panic won't help. Tell me EXACTLY what has happened. Stand up

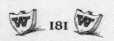

181

straight and stop that ridiculous crouching, do!'

'Oh, YES,' said Wellington, with such an enormous sigh of relief that one of the bulbs on the wall actually flickered. 'Oh, I AM glad you're back.'

'Quite right too. What's your report, eh?'

It was not quite as bad as Great Uncle Bulgaria had at first feared. There had, he gathered, been a further and sudden sinking, but fortunately no Womble had been injured, although there had been a great deal of shouting.

'*Shouting?*' said Great Uncle Bulgaria.

'It was very scaring, you know.'

'Ho-hum, I see. Continue.'

A great many doors had become jammed, the electric wiring had come loose and part of the Workshop and the kitchens were now out of order. Madame Cholet was at this moment serving hot snacks and drinks from the trolley and Tomsk was propping up a bulging ceiling in the Operations Room.

'And?' said Great Uncle Bulgaria – as Wellington hesitated. 'Brush down your fur, young Womble, there's no advantage in looking grey before you have to.'

'Yes, sorry,' said Wellington, slapping away at his coat which was covered in dust from the crumbling plaster. 'And I think I may have found somewhere we can go quickly. I remembered it sort of from when I was Librarian, before I was SD 3 that is; and I looked it up again and then, after Tomsk told me about Green Park and seeing, or at least *feeling*, all that wildlife, it occurred to me . . .'

'Ho-hum,' said Great Uncle Bulgaria. 'It occurs to *me* that you've been through rather a rough time, young Wellington, and that the best thing we can do is to find somewhere in the burrow which has *not* sunk – I trust there *is* such a place?'

Wellington nodded violently, sending a cloud of cement powder in all directions.

'To hold a proper meeting,' said Great Uncle Bulgaria calmly. 'Lead on, and there's no need to run.'

It was quite astonishing, but the moment Great Uncle Bulgaria re-entered the burrow all the rushing about and the shouting and the panic seemed to vanish and, as he moved at his usual slow pace through the passages, a kind of calm descended on the Wombles, so that by the time they had all gathered in the Playroom not even the smallest of them was afraid.

'Dear, dear, *dear* me,' said Great Uncle Bulgaria, putting on both pairs of spectacles. 'What a sorry-looking lot you are. *Tsk, tsk, tsk.*'

Something, which might almost have been a ripple of laughter, ran round the room and bulging ceilings and passages with holes in them suddenly seemed almost ridiculous.

'Ho-hum,' said Great Uncle Bulgaria, hitching his old tartan shawl more closely round his shoulders and nodding to Madame Cholet, who began to pass cartons of hot blackberry juice down the lines of Wombles from her trolley.

'There is nothing to be afraid of, you know. I'm here. I'll look after you. What a very silly lot of Wombles you are, to be sure,' said Great Uncle Bulgaria in quite a stern kind of voice, at which several of them looked at their paws and shuffled. 'In fact,' he went on, 'you hardly deserve the honour, the Very Great Honour which was bestowed on us this morning. However, when we are nicely settled in our New Home I shall tell you all about *that*!'

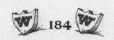

'Our New Home?' asked Tomsk.

'Yes, indeed. Thank you, Madame Cholet,' Great Uncle Bulgaria took the steaming carton which had been handed up to him and smiled, 'our New Home. Thanks to the work, the great work which has been done by Wellington, we shall soon, almost immediately in fact, be moving to a most important burrow. A burrow, moreover, where there is much work to be done and where we can be extremely useful.'

Great Uncle Bulgaria was well into his stride now and several of the older Wombles grew even more relaxed as they realised that a speech was about to be delivered, while the younger members of the community, quite worn out by the upheavals of the last few hours, began to doze, lulled by the comforting sound of Great Uncle Bulgaria's voice. If he was aware of their small, round heads drooping on to each other's shoulders, Great Uncle Bulgaria gave no sign of it, apart from one sharp glance at Madame Cholet, who somehow managed to make her way into the middle of the front row where her very ample lap provided a most comfortable resting place.

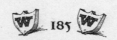

'...during the last few years Human Beings have grown even more untidy and wasteful and in the Centre of this Great City we are, therefore, more needed than ever before...'

'...zzzzzz ...' murmured the smallest Wombles.

'...it is obviously our duty to do what we can to help, and to see that not only their Commons but also their Parks are kept in a clean and pleasant condition...'

'...zzzzzzzzz ...'

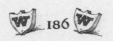

'So at 01.00 hours, that is,' Great Uncle Bulgaria corrected himself as he realised that none of the Wombles present, except Madame Cholet, Wellington and Tomsk, would know what he meant, 'at one o'clock tomorrow morning we shall start moving out of the burrow and into our new quarters.'

'How?' asked Wellington.

'Where?' asked Tomsk.

'By paw. Hyde Park.'

At this a general buzz of conversation broke out and Great Uncle Bulgaria let everybody talk, as he knew that there's nothing like a nice friendly discussion to clear the air; and it also gave him the chance to have a reviving sip of blackberry juice. He had carefully avoided any reference to Tobermory, Miss Adelaide, Bungo and Orinoco, as he didn't want to start the Wombles worrying about them.

'But what will happen to Wimbledon Common?' asked somebody in the back row. 'The Human Beings will never be able to manage without us to clear up after them.'

'I'm glad you asked me that question,' said

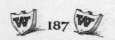

Great Uncle Bulgaria. 'It was a point which has been worrying me. However, the solution is simple. Some of us will return at a later date and move into the smaller, older burrow to the south of this one. It is further away from Tibbet's Corner and the heavy lorries, and therefore perfectly safe. Any Womble who would prefer to come back here should sign the paper which will be found pinned to the door.'

'Does this mean that we shall be splitting up?' asked Tomsk, looking very worried.

'Not at all. It merely means that we shall be spreading our net – perhaps I should say our "baskets and tidy-bags" – further.'

There was another rumble of laughter at this and Great Uncle Bulgaria raised one white paw and allowed himself a slight smile.

'We are and always shall be a very united family of Wombles. Our work may take us to – ho-hum – fresh fields and pastures new . . .'

'But that's our secret password . . .' said Tomsk and was given a hearty kick on the back paw by Wellington.

'But, even if we reach the heights of Hampstead

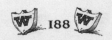

and the forests of Epping, Outer Bromley or,' and Great Uncle Bulgaria bowed slightly, 'the Royal grounds of Windsor, we must never forget that we are the Wombles of Wimbledon Common. And every year we shall be united, as a family, at our Midsummer party. That is all I have to say. Now you may all dismiss. We shall all gather again at 21.00 hours, at nine o'clock that is, for final orders.'

'Well,' said Tomsk.

'Um,' said Wellington, scribbling away in his notebook, 'hold on a tick, there's a good Womble.'

So Tomsk waited patiently until Wellington had finished his notes and shut up his book, by which time the Playroom was empty.

'Look here,' said Tomsk in his slow way, '*I* don't want to leave Wimbledon Common. There's a very good golf course, you know, and I've just got my handicap down to . . .'

'You don't have to leave it, you great gormless Womble. You can move into the deeper burrow later on,' explained Wellington.

'Oh, that's all right then,' said Tomsk with a happy sigh. 'But what about you, Wellington? What will you do?'

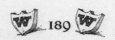

'I'll go for good, I think. You see, I sort of found the new place in Hyde Park, at least on those old maps, I did. Oh dear, I do hope they'll be all right – suppose they've all fallen in or vanished or something. It'll be my fault and . . .'

'Get away with you,' said Tomsk, towering over his friend and giving him a slap that almost sent him flying. 'You're a clever sort of Womble, you are. You're always right.'

'Ho-hum,' said Wellington, very pleased with this unexpected praise, but not at all sure that it was deserved. 'Well, we'll see . . .'

During the next few hours, the burrow was an absolute hive of industry as the Wombles scurried in all directions. After living there for so long, longer than any of them, even Great Uncle Bulgaria, could remember, it seemed extraordinary that they were going to leave. There was so much to be done: wiring to be disconnected and stores to be packed and lists to be made and things to be collected and everything to be sorted out. Even the smallest Womble was kept on the go, until at last everything was done, and they were all standing in line with a suitcase or bag or paper carrier clutched in each paw and a coat of some sort slung over every shoulder.

Their eyes were bright and their fur showed a tendency to stand on end as Great Uncle Bulgaria appeared round the corner of the now badly sloping passage. He was wearing the jacket and cap with the red stuff on it, and under his arm was the old plaid shawl and the great atlas from which every working Wimbledon Womble had chosen his or her name. Behind him was Madame Cholet, with her favourite cooking pans and a large casserole all neatly arranged on the trolley, and after her came Wellington with the big maps neatly rolled up, and his notebook, and the lantern with WBC on it, which he couldn't quite bear to part with. And last of all there was Tomsk, who had Great Uncle Bulgaria's rocking chair on his back, and the electric fire which Tobermory had made under one arm and his own golf clubs under the other.

Because of the way in which the Common had subsided most of Tobermory's electric lights were flickering on and off, and this had a strangely ghostly effect on the Wombles so that one moment their bright, watchful eyes could be seen quite clearly and the next they were like tiny gleaming candles.

'Wombles of Wimbledon,' said Great Uncle Bulgaria, his own two pairs of spectacles glinting, 'we are about to start on one of the greatest adventures of our lives. We look forward to a great and glorious future. Follow me!'

And he raised one white paw and then, without a backward glance, he began to march slowly but steadily towards the main door where Tomsk had so often worked as Nightwatch Womble. Everybody followed him, a little frightened perhaps, but each of them quite certain that whatever Great Uncle Bulgaria said was right.

Except, that is, Tomsk.

'Look here,' he said, waiting for the last Womble to leave the burrow as he had been instructed to do, so that he could switch off the last of the emergency lights. 'I say, Wellington.'

'Yes,' said Wellington, who was the last Womble but one.

'What about Tobermory and Miss Adelaide and Bungo and Orinoco, you know,' said Tomsk.

'They'll be all right,' said Wellington, carefully

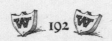

shutting the door as much as he could, which wasn't easy as it was now very crooked. And with these words he turned and pinned up a small notice which said:

> *Gone to Hyde Park.* FF *and* PN.
> *Scouts will be posted. Report as soon as possible.*
> *Signed:* BCW, OC, OWW
> P.S. *Look forward to seeing you.*

'Oh, that's all right then,' said Tomsk, sighing with relief.

''Course it is,' said Wellington. 'Look sharpish, old thing, or we'll get left behind. Come on now, quick march!'

And the two young Wombles set off at a fast jog trot across Wimbledon Common after the tail end of the last of the Wandering Wombles.

CHAPTER 14

The New Burrow

It was not, of course, to be expected that everything should go entirely smoothly, as it is no small thing to move a whole colony of Wombles across London from Wimbledon Common to Hyde Park without anything going wrong. Even at one o'clock in the morning there are still quite a number of Human Beings about and several of them, particularly policemen, were a bit startled. One of

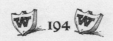

them went so far as to stop Great Uncle Bulgaria on Albert Bridge.

'Sorry, officer,' said Great Uncle Bulgaria who was, naturally, at the head of his troops, 'I suppose we should have stopped marching as this is a suspension bridge.'

'Yes,' said the policeman doubtfully, as he looked at a long line of Wombles, none of whom he could see very clearly as they were all in shadow, 'I dare say you should, but if I may . . .'

'Troops,' roared Great Uncle Bulgaria, 'stop marching.'

Which of course meant nothing to the Wombles, bar Tomsk, but which, however, gave Great Uncle Bulgaria time to use the information that he had acquired from the Buckingham Palace Gardens scouting party.

'I'm OC, OWW,' he said in a low voice as the Wombles began to amble over the bridge. 'Top Secret, of course. But I expect you'll have been told about us, eh?' And he laid one white paw knowingly against the side of his nose.

The policeman looked down at Great Uncle Bulgaria's cap and jacket with the red bits of

material on it and after a moment nodded wisely.

'Ah yes,' he said, 'quite, yes.'

'Good evening, officer,' said Great Uncle Bulgaria. 'Very mild for the time of year, isn't it? Ho-hum.'

It was five o'clock in the morning before the last of the Wombles had arrived in Hyde Park. They were all very sleepy by this time and as for Wellington, he was like a jelly, because for the last two hours he had been having terrible doubts as to whether what he had discovered in the old papers and books in the library (Operations Room) was right after all.

'Well?' said Great Uncle Bulgaria, gazing serenely over the calm waters of the Serpentine.

'Oh, I do HOPE so,' said Wellington, undoing one of the maps he'd been carrying under his arm. His paws were trembling so much he had to get Tomsk to help him while all the other Wombles, quite worn out by the journey, flopped down on the grass and looked around at this strange place which for most of them was to be their new home. Even the older ones had to admit that it was certainly extremely beautiful, for the land rolled up and down in gentle slopes, there were a great number of really high trees for climbing and a splendid stretch of water with an elegant bridge over it which made a perfect diving platform.

However, as their first loyalty must be with their old burrow, they only murmured between themselves 'not bad' and 'seems pleasant enough' and 'dare say we shall get used to it in time . . .'

'Th-there,' said Wellington, pointing to a spot he had ringed in red on the map. 'That's as near as I can place the old burrow. It's mentioned in a kind of book that I found in the library and . . .'

'I remember, I remember,' said Great Uncle Bulgaria, quite forgetting where he was for the moment as he looked back mistily into the past when he was a very young Womble. 'Great-great-great Uncle Hohenzollern's *Womble History of the World*. We were made to study it in the Womblegarten and very dry stuff we thought it too.'

'Suppose it's not true,' said Wellington who was getting more and more nervous by the second. In another three hours the Human Beings would start getting up and going to work, and the

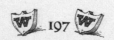

Wombles would be trapped in the middle of Hyde Park and would have to go into hiding until night-fall.

'If it's written by a Womble then it *must* be true,' said Great Uncle Bulgaria. 'Here, you say? Come along then and you too, Tomsk. The rest of you can stay here and have a snack. We shan't be long.'

Tidy-bags, baskets and suitcases were gratefully opened as the old Womble slowly made his way across the grass with Wellington and Tomsk following him. Not for the world would Great Uncle Bulgaria have admitted that he himself was very slightly apprehensive, for after all this was a very long shot. He merely straightened his shoulders, ignored the tired ache in his paws and presented a serene face to the world.

'Th-th-th . . .' stammered Wellington, who was now beyond plain speech.

'There,' said Great Uncle Bulgaria. 'I see,' and he began to prod about with his stick while the other two shifted from paw to paw and tried to stop their teeth from chattering with nerves.

'Ah-HA. Ho-hum,' muttered Great Uncle Bulgaria. 'Give me a paw, young Wombles.'

It was more than sight and touch that had made him find the correct place. It was deeply buried Womble instinct which showed itself in a kind of quiver which ran through all his white fur. It was like a long forgotten memory stirring into life, so that when Wellington and Tomsk, digging like furies, suddenly found themselves looking at a neat, round door most beautifully hidden from the outside world, Great Uncle Bulgaria was apparently not in the least surprised.

'A fine piece of craftsmanship that,' he said approvingly.

Tomsk and Wellington became aware that this was a Great Moment and solemnly stood aside as Great Uncle Bulgaria turned the handle and pushed. The door swung open, squeaking slightly, and the old Womble stepped inside, turning on his torch. The other two, unable to hang back any longer, hurried in after him, almost stepping on his back paws in their excitement. It was strange and a little scaring, and yet somehow very comforting, to discover this ancient burrow which had been built and inhabited by their distant Womble ancestors. They had certainly made a good job of it.

'What craftsmanship,' Great Uncle Bulgaria murmured over and over again as the light of the torch showed beautifully carpentered doors, slender arched roof supports and flagstone floors. And even those two very modern young Wombles, Tomsk and Wellington, let out 'oooos' of admiration when one particularly fine double door was opened and they saw before them what had obviously once been the Common Room.

'Oh MY!' they said together, staring about them at the carved rafters and the furnishings. 'Oh MY!'

'Sheraton, Chippendale, a sedan chair, a seventeenth-century clock, two Ming vases, early Rockingham,' murmured Great Uncle Bulgaria as he touched each object with a delicate paw. 'What taste they had. Ah, you just don't see work like that these days . . .'

'Is it all very valuable?' asked Wellington in an awed voice while Tomsk stood perfectly still, frightened to move a paw in case he brushed against something.

'It is now,' said Great Uncle Bulgaria. 'I presume that when these earlier Wombles were tidying up this Park – or open land it must have been in their day – these objects were not accounted of any great value. The Human Beings then must have dumped old bits of furniture much in the same way as they do today. Only now it's mostly gas stoves and hideous sofas and rusty bathtubs.'

'Will they become valuable in the future?' asked Wellington in surprise.

'I doubt it. Of course most of these things have been repaired, as you can see if you look very closely. All the same, with the way prices have risen in the antiques market, I should say that these are worth a great deal of money. But we mustn't stand here all day admiring them,' Great Uncle Bulgaria went on somewhat unfairly as he was the one who was doing the most admiring. 'There's work to be done. First, I must find one small room which I can use for further planning. This Grand Hall will be out of bounds until the contents have been properly catalogued. Wellington, put a notice on the door to that effect, but under no circumstances stick a pin into the wood. It must not be harmed!'

'Sir,' said Wellington, wondering how on earth he was going to do it without pinning. However,

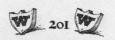

some earlier Womble must have had the same problem, for when he had written the words on a page from his notebook and had a closer look at the door, he saw that it had a small knocker, black from lack of cleaning, and he was able to wedge the notice securely under that.

'Come along, come along,' called Great Uncle Bulgaria who was now very eager to show this magnificent burrow to everyone else. 'Good gracious me!'

The light of the torch was directed at one wall of a small, somewhat bare room which held only a trestle table and a wooden stool.

'What is it?' asked Tomsk anxiously, afraid that they might have run into some awful drawback.

'There, my good Womble, there . . .'

The torchlight jumped up and down impatiently and Tomsk leant forward to take a closer look at whatever it was that was making Great Uncle Bulgaria lose his usual calm.

'It's only a lot of old drawings,' said Tomsk slowly. '*I* can draw better than that!'

'Ha!' said Great Uncle Bulgaria. 'Can you

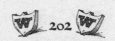

indeed! Those, you great gormless creature, are early Womble cave drawings! Look at that small Womble there with his paws full of bits and pieces – why, they must have been tidying up this part of London before there *was* any London. Amazing! To think that on and off this burrow has been in use for thousands and thousands of years. What a feeling of continuity it gives one.'

Tomsk frowned more than ever, staring intently at the faint marks of the paintings. Even if it *had* been drawn so long ago, it still wasn't very good to his way of thinking. The Womble had such long fur for one thing.

'I wonder why they left this burrow the last time?' said Wellington.

'Perhaps we shall never know,' Great Uncle Bulgaria replied. 'At the moment, however, it is not an important question. This will be my new Operations Room. Tomsk, you go and fetch the others. Wellington, get out your notebook. There's a lot to be done. A lot to be done!'

And Great Uncle Bulgaria sat down on the stool, with a sigh of relief at getting the weight off his paws, and stood the torch upright on the trestle table and began to dictate his very first orders from the new burrow.

There *was* a very great deal to be done as they all soon discovered, for, although the burrow was certainly grander than their old home, it was not at all as cosy or comfortable. Poor Madame Cholet nearly had a fit when she saw the kitchen quarters, but after her first shiver of horror, she set to work getting out her big apron and ordering a band of small Wombles here, there and everywhere, as she began to prepare the first meal.

'Oh, for my nice modern oven, oh, for my larders and the deep freeze,' she muttered to herself. 'Oh, if only Tobermory were here!'

A wish that was in every Womble's mind, for Tobermory had a way of sorting out problems with apparently no trouble at all, and, until he arrived, there could only be cold meals and all the lighting they had was paraffin lamps (Wellington was now especially delighted that he'd brought his WBC lantern) and torches.

Nevertheless, in spite of all the difficulties, some kind of order was produced and within two weeks of settling in the first Womble tidying-up parties were at work in Hyde Park and Kensington Gardens. The amount of stuff they brought back raised everybody's spirits considerably.

'Astonishing,' murmured Great Uncle Bulgaria as Tomsk proudly displayed an almost new and very expensive car rug, three pairs of gloves, six books, a camera, a heap of bus tickets, a mound of cartons and packets and several newspapers, including yesterday's edition of *The Times*.

'It is a lot, isn't it?' Tomsk agreed wonderingly.

'Yes, indeed. There's no news of Tobermory and party, I suppose?'

'No, but there are Wombles posted at every gate. It won't be long now, will it, Great Uncle Bulgaria?'

'No, no, of course not. Any day now, young Womble, any day now . . .'

But the days slipped past without any sign of the Scottish scouting party and, although Great Uncle Bulgaria tried to stop them, rumours began spreading through the burrow and many a head was shaken with a despondent sigh, as Womble sadly said to Womble, 'They won't be coming back . . . something bad must have happened to them . . .'

'Do you really think they are lost for ever?' asked Madame Cholet as she brought Great Uncle Bulgaria his (cold) evening dandelion drink.

'Not for ever,' he said slowly, 'no Womble just vanishes. Remember how Yellowstone ran away from Wimbledon Common all those years ago? Well, he came back in the end, didn't he? Even if it was only for a visit. We must take into account that Miss Adelaide and Tobermory have to *find* Bungo and Orinoco before they can return to London, and the Highlands are a big place. It's strange the way things happen, you know . . .'

'Yes,' prompted Madame Cholet as Great Uncle Bulgaria fell silent.

'Hmm? Oh, well, I was reading in *The Times* yesterday – how splendid it is to be absolutely sure of a copy *every* day – that there's been a report from the Highlands about a certain change in the behaviour of the wild animals up there. A kind of unrest, as though they had been disturbed slightly. I can't help wondering . . .'

'Yes, yes.'

'No, four Wombles on their own couldn't cause anything like that. They might startle a couple of

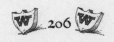

deer or a rabbit or two or even a golden eagle, but they wouldn't, couldn't, affect a whole large area like the Highlands. I wonder what *has* caused it?'

Great Uncle Bulgaria's curiosity was soon to be satisfied, but, as he didn't know that of course, he decided to try and calm the worries of the Wombles by putting up a suggestion box as to where they should hold their Midsummer party this year. Naturally all the Wombles who had signed the paper saying they wished to return to Wimbledon Common one day, wrote *Wimbledon Common*. There were several votes for Regent's Park, one (from Wellington) advocating the gardens at Buckingham Palace and a number who were in favour of repeating a trip to Battersea funfair, where they had once had a most successful outing. The majority, however, feeling that they had had enough wandering for a while, were solidly behind the idea of having a midnight boating party on the Serpentine with races, water sports and a diving competition from the bridge.

Great Uncle Bulgaria was going through all these suggestions and putting them into neat piles one evening, when suddenly there was a loud

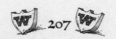

knocking on the door of the Operations Room.

'Come in, come in,' said Great Uncle Bulgaria rather crossly. He was becoming increasingly short-tempered these days, owing to his growing anxiety about his old friend Tobermory.

'Sir,' said Tomsk, throwing open the door and clicking his heels. 'Fresh Fields and Pastures New. SD 6 reporting, sir!'

'Eh?' said Great Uncle Bulgaria. 'You silly great gormless chuckle-headed thick-skulled creature. All that's over and done with now.'

And indeed Great Uncle Bulgaria had hung away his coat and hat with the red trimmings and gone back to his tartan shawl, which was now very shabby and didn't keep out the draughts which swept through the burrow if there was any wind.

'Sir!' repeated Tomsk, now grinning from ear to ear. 'SD 2, 4, 5 and 7 to see you. *Sir!*'

Great Uncle Bulgaria reached up a slightly trembling white paw to put on both pairs of spectacles and got very slowly to his feet. Wellington's notebook crashed to the floor and then for a moment there was silence.

'Good evening, Bulgaria,' said Miss Adelaide, appearing in the doorway.

'Hallo, old friend,' said Tobermory, looming up behind her.

'It's us, it's us,' shouted Bungo and Orinoco together, quite unable to hang back and play this game for one moment more.

'So I see,' said Great Uncle Bulgaria not quite steadily. 'Well, come in, come in, don't just stand there.' And he blew his nose very hard and then polished both pairs of spectacles and put them on and took them off again and shook everybody's paw several times over and said, 'Ho-hum, ho-hum,' very rapidly.

'Well,' said Tobermory, when at last some kind of order had been restored and Madame Cholet had brought in some sandwiches and a cake which she had really meant to keep for the outing, but even that seemed unimportant now, as she told Miss Adelaide at least six times.

'What do you think of our new home?' asked Great Uncle Bulgaria.

'Not bad,' said Tobermory. 'Good foundations, well laid. Any traffic trouble?'

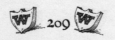

'No. Lorries of ANY KIND are forbidden to drive through the Park.'

'That's something, I suppose. Hallo, this dandelion tea's cold.'

'If you could only see my kitchens . . .' said Madame Cholet, shaking her head mournfully.

'Ho-hum, *tsk, tsk, tsk*,' said Tobermory, getting out his notebook and starting to make a neat list. 'No electricity either, and bad draughts. Yes, there's a great deal to be improved.'

'Not tonight though,' said Miss Adelaide, whose sharp eyes had noticed how careworn and thin Great Uncle Bulgaria looked even though he was now very happy. 'Which reminds me, we brought you a small gift from our Scottish cousins of the Clan MacWomble – a new Womble tartan shawl.'

'Wait till we tell you about them,' Bungo whispered to Wellington and Tomsk. 'And the Water-Wombles and the Clan Gathering and . . .'

'We ate for four hours without stopping,' said Orinoco, nodding his head. 'Four whole hours,' and he rubbed his stomach in happy memory.

'Now then, now then, not quite so much noise,' said Great Uncle Bulgaria. 'Well, Tobermory, can we get this place in good running order, do you think?'

Tobermory scratched one ear with his screwdriver, looked at his notes and then at Bungo, who was bursting with eagerness to tell Wellington and Tomsk of all their adventures.

'Well, Bungo, Orinoco,' said Tobermory with his slow smile, 'we did it for the MacWomble, didn't we? His burrow was very much like this. They had no idea of comfort, no idea at all. Still, by the time we left they weren't too bad, were they?'

'They were much improved,' said Miss Adelaide, nodding.

Bungo and Orinoco pushed each other, exchanged glances and then said solemnly in chorus, 'Och aye, they were that, Tobermory, they were that!'

CHAPTER 15

Great Uncle Bulgaria Looks Ahead

And so the Wandering Wombles of Wimbledon Common slowly, but with increasing comfort, settled into their new home under Hyde Park. Tobermory and Miss Adelaide both added their names to the list of Wombles who wished to return to Wimbledon to take over the small burrow which was furthest away from the main road and Tibbet's Corner. But none of them wanted to

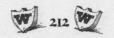

make the return move until after the Midsummer outing on the Serpentine.

Great Uncle Bulgaria was sad at the idea of parting from his old friends, but, as Tobermory pointed out, they would be able to meet regularly by using WOM I. They had given the motor scooter to the MacWomble as a parting gift, together with the overalls, binoculars, camera, film, crash helmets and scarves which were even now decorating the walls of that much improved Scottish hall, along with the Highland flags and banners. The MacWomble had been extremely pleased with his present and had learnt to ride it very quickly, as he meant to pay return calls on all the other Womble Chiefs; and was planning to travel as far north as Cape Wrath to make a courtesy visit to a very, very old Womble, Chieftain Fashven, who was one of the few left who could speak pure Womble Gaelic.

Bungo, Orinoco, Wellington and Tomsk all tried to outdo each other by telling increasingly extravagant stories about their adventures, in which each of them was, of course, the big bold hero. Some of these stories reached the ears of Great

Uncle Bulgaria and Tobermory and made them laugh very much indeed.

'Oh, well, they're only young,' said Great Uncle Bulgaria, wiping his eyes with the corner of his new MacWomble tartan shawl, which was the same tartan of course as the kilt worn by Cairngorm the MacWomble the Terrible, 'and they have been through a hard time. An exacting time. Indeed when I think of the perils, the lurking dangers, the . . .'

'Ah-HEM,' said Tobermory, gazing over the starlit

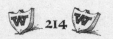

waters of the Serpentine and wondering if young Wellington had fully grasped exactly how to do the running repairs on the new deep freeze.

'I shall write my memoirs this winter,' said Great Uncle Bulgaria. 'The high point of which will be that Certain Matter which I mentioned to you.'

'Certain . . . ? Oh, you mean what She told you?'

'Yes. To think that we have the honour, the very GREAT honour to have been given a Warrant and made Parks and Commons Tidiers by Appointment to . . .' Great Uncle Bulgaria's voice grew husky and he had to clear his throat. 'I shall announce it to all our Wombles at the outing. I shall refer *particularly* to young Wellington and his magnificent work in finding our new home. Some kind of presentation, do you think? A medal perhaps?'

'Hmm,' said Tobermory. He'd had a long, hard day working on the new kitchens, and he was in no mood for a speech by his old friend. 'There's a lot to think about.'

They both were silent for a moment; and then Great Uncle Bulgaria straightened his old shoulders and rested one white paw on Tobermory's grey arm.

Tomsk, who had just come on duty as Night-watch Womble, opened the door for them and ticked their names off on his list.

''Night, young Womble,' said Great Uncle Bulgaria. 'Well, I'm off to bed, Tobermory, old friend, and you look as if you could do with a good night's rest too. First thing in the morning I shall start putting Wellington's notes in order for my memoirs. I shall call them *Operation Wandering Womble* or perhaps, even more simply, *The Wandering Wombles*.'

'Shall I be in it?' asked Tomsk hopefully. It would be very important to have your name in a book.

'Of course you will,' said Great Uncle Bulgaria, 'we all will.'

And smiling thoughtfully to himself, Great Uncle Bulgaria walked slowly down the now electrically lit passage to his bed, while Tomsk carefully rebolted the main front door of their new home under Hyde Park.

The Wombles Who's Who

MADAME CHOLET...

... is a brilliant Womble cook and her blackberry and apple pie is famous throughout Wombledom. She is very inventive and can turn her paw to any recipe, using ingredients the young Wombles gather on the Common. She is very kind but can get cross when young Wombles interrupt her cooking, especially Orinoco!

TOMSK...

... is the largest of the young Wombles and is very good at sport. He may not be good at reading or

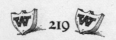

writing but he is brilliant at getting Wombles out of tight spots when a bit of strength is called for.

ORINOCO ...

... is the fattest, greediest and laziest of the young Wombles. His favourite job is 'helping' Madame Cholet to taste recipes in the kitchen. He doesn't like tidying-up duties on the Common and usually finds a bush to hide behind and have a nap, saying, 'I'll just have a nice forty winks'. Quite often he is woken up by another Womble's adventure.

BUNGO ...

... is the youngest of the working Wombles. Even though he has not been on tidying-up duties as long as the other young Wombles, he is rather bossy and thinks he knows the answer to everything. He's usually wrong! Great Uncle Bulgaria sometimes looks at him over the top of his spectacles and says, 'Bungo! Silly sort of name, but it suits him'.

TOBERMORY ...

... is extremely clever with his paws and runs the

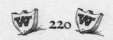

Womble Workshop. The young Wombles bring him all kinds of rubbish and broken objects that they find on the Common. Tobermory takes off his bowler hat, scratches his head for a moment, and then mutters, 'Problems, problems', before turning the rubbish into something very useful.

GREAT UNCLE BULGARIA . . .

. . . is over 300 years old and is the wisest of the Wimbledon Wombles. To keep warm he wears a MacWomble tartan shawl, and his favourite newspaper is *The Times*. Great Uncle Bulgaria can be strict and turn a young Womble into jelly when he looks at them over the top of his spectacles and says, '*Tsk, tsk, tsk*, young Womble'. However, he is also very kind and it is to him that the Wombles turn for help and guidance.

ALDERNEY . . .

. . . is a pretty young Womble who is in charge of the burrow's tea trolley. As the Wombles love their food this is an important job which she enjoys. Alderney is also a bit headstrong and can lead other young Wombles into scrapes.

COUSIN YELLOWSTONE . . .

. . . lives in the Yellowstone Park burrow in the USA. His full name is Yellowstone Boston Womble and he's very well dressed, kind-hearted and quite old, with silky grey fur. He left the Wimbledon burrow when he was young and sailed all over the world until he settled in the USA.

WELLINGTON . . .

. . . is rather shy, very clever and he is the smallest of the Wombles. He loves reading, inventing things and helping Tobermory in his Workshop. Some of Wellington's inventions are really very good but he always apologises for them!

CAIRNGORM, THE MACWOMBLE THE TERRIBLE . . .

. . . lives in the Scottish burrow by Loch Ness in Scotland, where he helps to look after Nessie the Water-Womble. He often visits the Wimbledon burrow, where he drives everyone mad by playing the bagpipes. Cairngorm can be quite gruff and even bossier than Bungo!

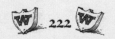

Wonderful Wombling Facts

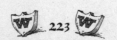 Wombles choose their names from places, cities and rivers found in Great Uncle Bulgaria's atlas of the world.

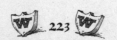 Young Wombles spend their time in the Womblegarten, run by Miss Adelaide Womble, until they are old enough to tidy up outside.

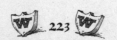 Midsummer's Eve is the most important night in the Wombles' year. They have a big party and eat far too much.

There are Womble burrows all over the world, including Hyde Park in London, Loch Ness in Scotland, Yellowstone Park in the USA, and the Khyber Pass on the border of Pakistan and Afghanistan. The main burrow is underneath Wimbledon Common, South-west London.

Fortune and Bason is Orinoco's favourite shop.

Great Uncle Bulgaria's middle name is Coburg.

The WOMBLES

Win your very own Wombles goody bag!

If you'd like the chance to enter the
free prize draw, email your name and address to
competition@thewomblesbooks.com.
Or send your name and address on a postcard to
The Wombles Competition, Bloomsbury
Publishing, 36 Soho Square, London, W1D 3QY.

Each month we will put the entries into Bungo's
hat and select one winner at random to receive
an **exclusive Wombles goody bag**.
Good luck!

Only one entry per child. The closing date for entries is 31st December 2011.
Terms and conditions apply.

See **www.thewomblesbooks.com** for details.

Welcome to the wonderful world of

The WOMBLES

Have you visited the Wombles website at **www.thewomblesbooks.com**?

There are games, activities and lots of fun things to do, as well as news and information about all of your favourite Wombles!

Join in the fun with your favourite Wombles

The Invisible Womble

Tobermory, DIY-er extraordinaire, gets to grips with one of the Human Beings' most ingenious inventions: the vacuum cleaner! But has he got it *quite* right?

The Wombles at Work

There has been a huge festival near the Wombles' burrow and no end of rubbish has been left behind – everything from umbrellas to shoes, drink cans and bottles. The Wombles have their work cut out for them . . .

COMING SOON!

Look out for more fantastic Wombling stories

The Wombles to the Rescue

The Human Beings have realised that they have an energy crisis and are throwing much less away, which has caused the Wombles' supplies to run dangerously low. What can the Wombles do? It's time for EMERGENCY SPECIAL PROJECTS – with DIY king Tobermory in charge!

The Wombles Go round the World

Great Uncle Bulgaria loves telling the younger Wombles all about the history of the many Womble clans. But the young Wombles find this rather boring! So Tobermory invents two clever clockwork air balloons and four young Wombles are sent on the adventure of a lifetime – around the world!

COMING SOON!

Don't miss the very first Womble adventure!

The Wombles

Bungo makes his very first trip to the Common. Large, noisy dogs and dangerously windy weather are just the beginning of this young Womble's adventures!

OUT NOW!

Carry on Wombling . . .
and collect all 6 books!

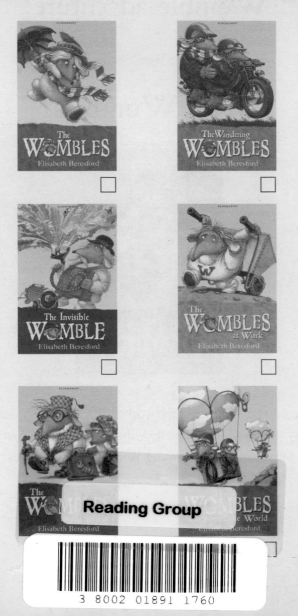